Sweat and Desire

Enemy to Lovers

Off-limit Romance

by:

Pebble James

<u>Chapter 1</u>

Jack

"Jack," my uncle Johnny hollered across the gym. "You made it!"

I strode to where my father's younger brother leaned against the fighting ring's rope and watched two fighters practicing. The noises reverberating through the warehouse building made me want to cover my ears. I never knew a Mixed Martial Arts' gym could be so loud. I knew fights, when in arenas, could be deafening, but this pandemonium and racket made me appreciate earplugs.

"Yeah, I made it," I hugged him, and we slapped each other's' back. "Later than I wanted to get here, but I'm here."

"Go to the body, go to the body," my uncle yelled at one of the fighters.

I watched the two fighters in the ring as the one my uncle yelled at stopped hitting his opponent in the head and focused on the other parts of the body. The fighter being pummeled on jerked back and side kicked the other fighter.

The first fighter fell back, but bounced up faster than anyone I'd ever seen.

"Good, good move, Lenny," my uncle clapped. "You gonna take that crap, Kyle? Move on him!" I watched as the two men sparred in the ring, and my excitement grew knowing I'd be out there in the ring soon battling it out with another fighter. I stood next to my uncle and hung my hands on the bottom rope. The noise from the other rings, fighters and trainers seemed to disappear as I focused on the two men in front of me.

"Ok, that's enough," my uncle shouted, clapping his hands. "Good round guys!"
He turned to size me up. His eyes traveled up and down my body. I'd been working out, eating a high protein diet and have developed some muscle over the last few months. It's been a year since I saw my Uncle Johnny. I told him of my interest in training to be an MMA fighter at his gym, the Rogue Warriors, and he laughed.

Not in a kind way, either. He laughed hysterically.

After he calmed down, he told me I needed to gain some weight and put some of the flab on my body into a tone muscle form.

"Yeah," he nodded. "I see you took my advice last year."

"I told ya I'm serious," I nodded. "Put on almost twenty pounds of muscle."

"Hmm," he raised an eyebrow. "We'll see..."

"Hey, Johnny!" someone yelled across the gym. "Gotta scheduling problem here!" "Yeah," he hollered back. "Coming! Go back to my office there." he tilted his head to the left. "Wait inside."

"Okay," I said and wandered in the direction he nodded. As I strode through the gym, I watched other fighters training, working out and talking. A few nodded at me, while most ignored my presence, as they're too focused on their activities. I stopped just outside my uncle's office and watched two female fighters dancing around the ring. Their coaches and other onlookers yelling, shouting and calling out to them.

The taller of the two women, a dirty blonde with her hair in tight braids close to her head, appeared to be a southpaw. She jabbed with her right hand, and throwing the harder punches with her left.

The shorter female seemed to be favoring the inside of the ring. She'd throw out quick punches and then a hook, but the tall blonde met every punch.

Impressive.

"Under, under!" a man standing outside the ring shouted. "Dammit, Rachel, under!"
"Shut the hell up, Manny," the tall blonde woman spit out her mouthpiece. "How the frick am I gonna go under when she's covering up!"

"That's it," the guy, Manny, held up his hands and stormed off.

"Fuck off," the blonde growled, and took off her headgear. She tossed it outside the ring and went to the other side of the ring from me. She grabbed a towel and wiped her face in it. She removed her gloves and let them fall to the ring's floor.

The first words that came to mind describing this woman were a *complete badass.* I guess all females who are MMA fighters could be called that, but this woman could be the poster child for it. Tattoos adorned her biceps and the nape of her neck. Her brow furrowed, and a cut was visible just above her left eyebrow. The blood trickled down towards her temple and when she wiped her face; the blood smeared. She picked up a small plastic trash can and spit into it. She wiped her mouth with the back of her hand. As she set, the can back down, her eyes met mine. I grinned, and she scowled. Definite attitude.

"Problem," she frowned.

"No," I didn't know what to say. I turned and went into Johnny's office. "Damn," I murmured once inside. I glanced back, and she still glared at me.

"Cripes," I whispered and walked around my uncle's office. Behind his desk, my uncle had a floor to ceiling shelving unit filled with trophies, awards and other framed certificates. I strolled over to the shelves and read some of the trophy titles. I saw a breakthrough fighter of the year from three years ago for Rachel Corvi, Bantamweight awards for a few other fighters and some framed magazine covers featuring the Rogue Warriors Gym.

I turned and glanced at the desk, which was a total disaster. Papers and folders strewn about and someone's headgear and fighting gloves sat in the middle of the paper tornado aftermath. "Sorry about that, Jack," my uncle strode into his office and shut the door.

"It's okay," I replied and sat on the sofa opposite of his desk. "So, here you are," he smiled at me. "I didn't think you were serious."

"I'm definitely serious," I nodded.

"It's a lot of hard work and bullshit to get you in shape," he said and sat on the edge of his desk. A few papers fell to the floor.

"I'm up for it," I replied. "I listened to your advice last year."

"Yeah, I see that," he nodded. "Whatcha up to now? One-eighty?"

"One-eighty-four," I said, grinning, proud of myself for gaining the weight I needed. "Good, good," he said and stood. "But hear me on this, just because you gained the weight and built some muscle doesn't mean you're up for this. It's a hard life. Lots of knock downs, and I don't mean in the ring. Every man and woman out there in the ring wants the championship, but only one gets it." He circled his desk and rummaged through some of the papers and folders. He took one of the folders and handed it to me. "Take this out to Manny, he's a cutman..."

"A what?" I asked and took the folder from him.

"The guy out there," Johnny pointed to the man that worked with the tall blonde. "He's our best cutman. He makes sure the fighters are good to go in the ring. Like a manager of sorts." "Oh, okay," I replied. "What's he gonna do for me?"

"He'll get you weighed in, get you some gear and get you settled in the gym," Johnny said. "Then come back here and I'll get you a trainer."

"Okay." I stood and headed out of the office.

"Hey, Jack," Johnny yelled to me. "Any preference on a trainer?

"No," I said. "Just give me the one that'll get me to the championship round."

"If only it was that easy," he laughed.

***

I spent an hour with Manny getting outfitted, trying on a good headgear and being weighed and evaluated. I felt like a guinea pig in a lab prepping for some kind of experiment. Manny wasn't a talkative guy, he was more of a grunter. Everything I said, or asked, he'd grunt. I don't understand grunt yet, so I figured it was a good thing Manny wasn't going to be my actual trainer. When we were done, I followed him out to the main gym and we walked across towards Johnny's office. He knocked on the door, opened it, and we walked in.

"He's set," Manny said.

"Thanks," Johnny replied.

"Find a trainer?" I asked and sat in the chair across from my uncle.

"Yeah," he said, "Rachel."

"A girl?"

"Don't let her hear you say that," he laughed. "She'll bust your ass before you can blink." "C'mon, Johnny, a girl, seriously?" I shifted in the chair. "I want someone who can take me to the top, not some girl."

"She's a Bantamweight champ," he stood. "And you better lose that chip on your shoulder. If not, you won't be here long."

I rolled my eyes.

"Everyone out there," he pointed to the gym, "is equal. Man or woman. Every person out there has a point to prove. You're no different. If you fuck up, someone will let you know. Most of these fighters have been at it for years, and if they know you walked your fucking ass in here making demands and have an attitude, they'll tear you apart."

"I get it," I hissed.
"Do you?" he replied. "Cause all I see is a kid looking for a title. Not

someone disciplined. You go into the cage acting like this, they'll kick your ass all the way back home. You think your life has been hard? Theirs have been worse. They don't screw around!"

We glared at each other.

"Isn't there another trainer available? Not sure how I feel about a girl."

"Dammit, Jack," Johnny hollered. "Rachel's your trainer. If you don't like it, there's the fucking door." He pointed to his office door.

I shook my head, frustrated, but knowing I lost the battle. "Fine, but if she doesn't produce, I want a new trainer!"

"Come on," he whipped the door open.

I followed him into the gym and he yelled for her.

"Rachel, c'mere!"

The tall blonde I watched earlier turned her head and climbed out of the ring where she was practicing, and jogged over to Johnny.

"Whatcha need?" she said and wiped her forehead with her gloved hand. She glanced my way and sneered.

"This here's my nephew, Jack," Johnny slapped my back. "I need you to take some time and get him set up."

She rolled her eyes. "Come on, Johnny. I have my own training."

"And you'll still have time for that," he promised. "He's just starting out, so it's the basics. Nothing too in-depth."

"Crap, Johnny," she wrung her hands together.

"Hey, you were him once," Johnny said.

She ran her eyes up and down my frame and laughed.

"I was never that scrawny." "True," my uncle joined in on the laughter.

"Hey, I'm right here, you know," I replied. "Geez..."

"Oh, shut up," Rachel shook her head. "What are you? A mama's boy?"

"No," I seethed. "I just don't like being the joke, okay?"

"You're not a joke," Johnny stepped in. "You're the new guy. You get the razzing from the other fighters. If you can't handle that, you need to ask yourself if you want to be a fighter or not." "Hell yeah, I want to be a fighter," I growled. "That's why I'm here."

"Then act like it," Rachel hissed. "You act like a mamsypamsy. We'll treat you like one." I balled up my hands and had the fists at my side. Rachel stepped closer.

"If you're gonna set them up," she nodded to my hands, "you best be ready to use them." "Hey, now," Johnny shook his head. "We're off to a terrible start."

Rachel stepped back, but we maintained eye contact, seeing who could out stare the other. "Rachel," Johnny held up a finger to her, "no mention of Jack's mother, or any reference to him being a mamma's boy."

I grinned. She sneered.

"Jack, don't provoke Rachel," he glanced at me. "She's doing a huge favor for me and you. You piss her off. I'm not responsible for what happens."

He glanced between the two of us. "Got it?"

We both nodded.

"Good," Johnny clapped his hand. "Now, train." He held out his hands, bowed and backstepped away.

I held Rachel's glare. I could tell she's fuming.

"Hey, I didn't pick you to train me," I said.

"Whatever," she snorted. "Follow me around today. I already have my time slot ready. Tomorrow we'll start early."

"How early?" I followed her when she started walking back to the ring.
"Five," she said, climbing up and slinked through the ropes.

"In the morning?" I squeaked.

"Keep it up and it'll be four," Rachel laughed.

Chapter 2

Rachel

I slammed a fist into Josh, my trainer's, hand. I was taking my aggression out in this practice from having to be a babysitter for Johnny's nephew. I am not a glorified babysitter. "Ugh," I yelled, kicking up and connecting my foot with Josh's gloved hand.

"Damn, girl," Josh hollered. "What's got into you today?"

"Juts some extra pent-up frustration," I said, bouncing around, getting my adrenaline under control.

"Damn, you keep that shit up, you'll kill it in the finals," Josh bellowed.

"I'll have to keep my motivation up then," I said, glancing at Jack.

I worked with Josh for the rest of the hour and felt pretty good until I turned around and saw Jack standing at the ropes. I tossed my head back, sighed and climbed out of the ring. "Damn," he said when I walked past him to get a towel. I wiped the sweat off my face as he kept talking. "How long have you been fighting?"

"Eight years total," I said, opening a bottle of water

and swallowing half the bottle. "Damn," he whistled.

"Is that the extent of your vocabulary?" I drank more water,

"No," he said.

I sat on a bench and eyed Jack. He was what some people would call a 'pretty boy'. He has that *just climbed out of bed* tussled look to his dark brown hair. There wasn't anything special about his brown eyes, except they reminded me of doe; big and round. He had that wholesome, small-town boy next door vibe going on.

For some reason, all those components irritated me.

The kid wasn't fighter material, in my opinion. He was too soft. Too naïve.

When I showed up at the Rogue Warrior years ago, I had attitude. I had sass. I was a force to be reckoned with.

This Jack fella wasn't anything like that. I imagined the only fight he had was someone cutting the line in front of him at the local ice cream shop. I snorted, thinking about that visual. "So, tomorrow, at five?" Jack asked.

"Yeah, five, don't be late," I stated. "You're late, you lose out."

"Got it," he saluted me and strolled away.

I watched him walk away. His lanky body had little muscle, or fat for that matter. He needed to gain some weight. There was no way he could hold his own in the ring if he was to enter one today. I wasn't holding much hope for Jack, even with all the training in the world.

I stood and went into the women's locker room and began the end of the day routine. Shower, dress and head home to my small loft apartment over the old garage in the gym's parking lot. Johnny let me live here with a reduced rent because when I first came to the Rogue Warrior, I literally had nothing. Only what I could fit into the cab of my two-decade old S-10 truck, which wasn't much. I left home when I was seventeen and wandered the state for a few years before I got a stable job.

But minimum wage barely covered the bills. I spent ten years being what some people call a nomad after I was evicted from a crappy apartment in a little town near the California and Oregon borders. I was first introduced to Martial Mixed Arts fighting when I knew a girl; I cleaned hotels with about a decade ago. She had a side job cleaning up the arena after a fight, and she knew I needed money, so when she asked if I wanted to make a quick hundred bucks. I

was in. We showed up after the fights were over and all the fans

had left. It was an eerie silence in the arena as we swept and

mopped the floor, wiped down the chairs and picked up garbage. I

was mesmerized by the ring and banners hanging from the ceiling.

I asked the girl about the MMA, and she shrugged, saying she was

just here to clean. She didn't have a clue what MMA was, nor did

she care.

I was interested and spent a few days at the local library using their

internet to learn what MMA was, and what happened. I was

fascinated that woman had their own division. From that moment on,

I was in search of a gym.

I ended up at Johnny's gym on a fluke. I had gone to a few other

gyms, but when the sexual innuendoes and shady fighters wanted

more from me for helping me train, I hightailed it out. I was sitting at

a bar about two miles from the Rogue Warrior when Johnny and some

of his fighters strolled in after a big win. *How was I to know this was*

their favorite bar to celebrate at? I waited until they were seated in

the corner booth, then I inquired with the bartender who the group of guys were. When he told me they were from the Rogue Warrior, my mind churned. I hadn't been to that gym and I stood, made my way over to their booth and introduced myself. Johnny invited me to join them. I jumped at the chance, and after a couple of hours, Johnny told me to stop by the gym in the morning. I shook his hand, telling him I'd be there bright and early. I was extra early the following morning, as I slept in my truck in the parking lot. I was woken up by Johnny knocking on my driver's side window. He said I couldn't sleep in my truck in his parking lot. I reminded him that he invited me to come by today to see his gym.

We walked into the gum, and he told me to come to his office. When I got in there, he opened his desk drawer and took out a key. He tossed it to me, told me to unpack in the small apartment over the garage, then come back in and we'd talk.

The rest, as they say, is history.

I grabbed my shower bag and headed into the shower rooms.

I was hungry, and I knew I had some money left in the bank. But not winning a fight in two years was taking its toll on my bank account. So, I tried to think about what I had in my refrigerator. Not much, as memory recalls. As I finished my shower and walked to my locker, I figured I'd go by the corner deli and see if they needed someone to make deliveries. It was Friday, so they may need an extra hand. I did that sometimes to compensate when the money was tight. The owner of the deli paid me for free sandwiches at the end of the night.

I was craving some extra carbs, and I also knew the deli would toss out the lettuce and tomatoes when I could use them. I love salad, and if I added some creamy salad dressing, my body's been craving not only the carbs but also the fats that's in salad dressing, I'd be content for a few days.

I got dressed in a pair of sweats and pulled my blonde hair up in a high ponytail. I grabbed my duffle bag and headed for my apartment. I dropped the bag inside the door, locked it up and decided to walk to the deli. It's only a few blocks and the evening was cool, but not too bad. I walked in and waved to the owner, Eddie. He nodded and smiled.

"Come to work for your dinner," he yelled out over the noise from the customers. "You know it," I said and slipped onto a stool near the register. "Got any orders needing to go out?"

"Sure do," Eddie hollered. "By the register. There's two."

Eddie's problem with keeping delivery people employed was my opportunity. He needed a
Delivery person. I needed food. *Win-win.*

I snatched up the two bags, checked the addresses and walked back to get my truck. I was back at the deli within ten minutes since both deliveries were closed. I went back inside, sat at the counter again and waited for the next order.

Sitting here, I had some time to think about training Jack. I've helped other trainers when they needed it, but I've never had control over training a person myself. I was excited that Johnny had faith in me, but I was resentful because I instantly disliked Jack, and his training would interfere with my own training. But telling Johnny no wasn't in the cards. I owed him so much, so this was the least I could do for him.

"Order up, Rachel," Eddie called from the kitchen.

Chapter 3

Jack

He pulled his decade-old sedan into the Rogue Warrior parking lot

and turned off the engine. I sat there, with only the street light

illuminating my surroundings. Cocking my head, I stared at the

graffiti painting all over the brick facade. Someone had taken their

time creating the images of four MMA fighters.

One of the fighters was my uncle, but I didn't know the other two

men. The only female on the wall had to be Rachel. Her stance, the

way the graffiti artist captured her facial features, dark blonde hair,

and what most people called the cauliflower ears.

The ears of every MMA, or other fighters for that matter, are created

from all the hits and blows to the ear. The trauma to the cartilage

causes blood vessels to burst and tissue damage. Having these

disfigured ears is a rite of passage.

My mind stayed on thoughts of Rachel as I stared at the wall. I can't

remember seeing her ears yesterday, maybe because I was too

focused on her being the woman Johnny had set me up with to train.

That still busted my balls. I wondered what other guys were subjected to a woman trainer. Regardless, I'd tell Johnny to give me a new trainer if I didn't see any positive results—a male trainer.

I removed the keys from the ignition and grabbed my duffle bag in the passenger seat. Empty water bottles, fast food bags, and other trash tumbled to the floorboard. I'd been living in this car for the last few months, and it was wearing thin.

It was annoying to shower at truck stops or campgrounds. My meals weren't too bad, as there was fast food everywhere on every corner, but most of my meals came from churches that offered a midday meal for free or lousy gas station food. Nothing is quite as appetizing as a hot dog turning on a roller for four hours.

Within the first month of being homeless, I learned that some gas stations, if you went in around midnight, were willing to give a person the old food because they had to clean the machines before, they closed for the night.

After getting settled here and having my first training session, I plan on talking to Johnny about somewhere to stay. I doubted I could live with him, as his new wife, Marie, didn't like me. She made that clear the last time I saw Johnny a year ago.

I had commented about Johnny's first wife, and Marie heard me, and she went off on me. That lady is a whack job. All I had said was I remembered how Aunt Jennie used to make a particular dessert. and how good it was when Marie started yelling and going off on a tangent.

Marie told me to leave her house, and when I looked to Johnny for help, he told his wife to calm down. Marie went off on him as well, and I chose to leave. My mom and Aunt Jennie were sisters, so Johnny was an uncle by marriage, and Marie commented that I was only at *her* house to get something from Johnny, which was a lie. Johnny would always be my uncle, regardless of his blood ties.

As I strolled across the parking lot, my thoughts went to my mom. I missed her every day. She'd turned to drugs when I was in junior high, and she never got off them until her death right before I turned sixteen. My Aunt Jennie was in no better shape, so Johnny and Jennie divorced.

Aunt Jennie just seemed to disappear as the divorce sent her over the edge. The last Johnny had seen her was in court when their divorce was granted. Johnny said she looked haggard and strung out. So, when my mom died, I had to go to the coroner's office to identify her, something no fifteen-year-old kid should ever have to do.

I grew up fast. I dropped out of high school and tried to survive in the house my mom and I lived in, but that only lasted two months before the landlord came by to talk to my mom. I broke down crying and told him she had died. I was evicted the following week. The landlord said it was because I was late with the rent, but he just wanted me gone.

I bounced from friend's house to friend's house for about a year before I overstayed my welcome. Eventually, I found a more consistent job with a landscaping company, and when I saved up enough money, I lived in a campground for the next year. I paid for one of the small one-room cabins, but at least I had electricity, running water, and a place to sleep every night.

When I lost my job with the landscaper, I was at square one again. Over the next five years, I stayed where I could, had odd jobs, and just lived life for the moment.

A year ago, when I visited Johnny and Marie, I was going to ask him for some guidance, but Marie made sure I didn't. I remember she'd been eyeing me all night, suspicion in her squinting eyes, as she kept assessing my every move.

I hooked up with a girl I met in a bar one night and lived with her for almost nine months. Then she booted me out when she found someone with a steady job.

To say my life has been rough is an understatement.

I opened the main door to the gym and walked inside. Some lights were on around the arena, and I could see Johnny's office light on. I didn't remember seeing his truck outside but figured I was distracted by the graffiti mural.

"Hey, *Johnny*," I hollered.

"In here," he yelled back.

I strode over to his office and leaned on the door frame. "Whatcha doin' here so early?" I asked. "Early?" He glanced at the clock on the wall. "I never went home."

"Didn't realize there's so much paperwork for you to deal with," I replied.

"Not paperwork," Johnny pushed back from his

desk. "Dealing with that bitch." "Marie?" I knew

the answer before even asking.

"She's a full-blown psycho." he ran a hand over his face.

As much as I wanted to tell him I knew that already, I didn't. No

sense in poking the bear when he's angry.

"She went off on me last night 'cause I was late," Johnny stood. "So,

I said, fuck it. You think this is late? Just wait."

I chuckled, crossed my arms over my chest, and watched him pour a

cup of coffee. He took a sip, staring out the window in his office that

overlooked the gym.

"You here to train?" He asked.

"Yeah," I mumbled. "Kinda early, but my drill sergeant said I had to be
here."

"Don't mock it," Johnny said, glanced at me, and gave me *the look*.

He warned me about the *girl* trainer issue I had been vocal about
yesterday.

"I know, I know," I held up my hands. "I'm not complaining about her
being a girl."
"I hope not," he drank more coffee. 'Cause I can't do that right now

again."

"No, I'm good." I held up my hands.

A door slamming shut echoed through the gym. I glanced over my shoulder and saw Rachel walking towards one of the cages. She had her duffle bag over her shoulder and dropped it on a bench. She glanced in my direction and nodded.

I nodded and looked at Johnny. "You gonna be, okay?"

"Yeah, just another day," Johnny snorted. He held up his coffee cup and saluted me. "Have fun." "Not supposed to be fun, is it?" I chuckled, pushed off the wall, and left the office. I trekked to where Rachel had set her bag down and sat on the bench. I watched as she wrapped

her hands with tape and prepared for the ring. I got out of my gear and began getting ready as well. "Morning," I said when she hadn't said anything.

"We'll see," she climbed into the cage

"Ready?" She pounded her gloved hands together.

"Almost," I replied.

"Day's not getting any earlier," she yelled. "Let's go."

"Are you always this pleasant first thing in the morning," I growled and climbed into the cage. "Yeah, and my personality goes downhill the longer I have to wait," she bounced between her feet, rolling her shoulders back to stretch some muscles. "We're only gonna be in here for a few minutes. I want to see what ya got."

I nodded and stood straight.

Rachel held her fisted hands in front of her, just like a boxer would do, and continued shifting on her feet. I raised my hands to mimic her and shuffled my feet to the right. Rachel didn't follow suit and remained in the same spot. I moved another step to the right.

"What the hell you doing? Dancing?" She laughed.

"You wanted to see what I got," I stopped moving.
"And that's it?" She shook her head. "Oh, brother."

"You're the teacher," I said. "So, teach me!"

"I don't know if there's enough *teach* in me for this," she raised her hands again. "Okay, come at me."

I raised my hands and shifted from foot to foot, then midway through a shift, I took my left hand and threw it at her. Rachel raised her right hand, blocked me, and pushed my hand back with her left hand.

"Come on," she yelled. "Come at me!"

"What the fuck?" I yelled.

I'm furious now. I raised my right hand to block and slammed my left into her chest. She jerked back and immediately threw her right fist at me, connecting with my jaw. She bounced back from my hit, and I'm not sure if I didn't hit her hard enough or if she was just that good.

"Gotta give as good as you get," she mocked me. "Now, come at me like you're pissed off!" "I AM pissed off," I shouted, my mouthpiece coming loose, and I spewed saliva. "Then act like it," she tossed her head back and laughed.

She held up her hands and moved to her left. I followed and moved. I closed the gap between us, threw my right hand, and collided with her chest. She stumbled back and regained her footing. "Yeah, come on, bring it," she yelled.

Before she could say another word, my left hand bolted out and slammed into her jaw. Her head jerked back, and she shook her shoulders.

"Better," she hollered.

We moved in a semi-circle, and I heard the gym's exterior door slam shut, announcing someone else had arrived. My first instinct was to glance over, and when I did, Rachel took that opportunity to strike me. Her right hand slammed into my chest, and I lost my balance. I staggered and fell to the mat. "Whoa, Rachel," a man yelled from outside the cage.

I glanced over and saw a dark-haired man resting his forearms on the rope. He was smiling at Rachel and clapped his hands. I didn't recognize the man from yesterday. He made eye contact with me, and the smile changed to a cocky smirk.

"You gonna take that shit from a girl?" He laughed. "Get up!"

"Shut up, man," I wiped my mouth, and blood trickled on my glove. I pushed up, rolled my shoulders, and turned to face Rachel. Instead of boasting, she was in her stance for retaliation. "Five more minutes," Rachel yelled. "See what else you can do!"

My fury was forefront, and I almost charged at her, but I held up my hands and moved toward her. We sparred for the next five minutes, with me getting a few good hits, but it was apparent that Rachel domineered over me.

By the time we were done, a small group of fighters and trainers were milling about. Some watched us, cheering Rachel on or cussing at me to *man up*. That shit pissed me off, and every time the first dark-haired man came into the gym, I got in my punches and strikes. Something about that guy goaded me.

When Rachel called the five minutes up, my adrenaline was high, and it took me a few minutes to calm down. Rachel grabbed us both a bottle of water, and I downed the entire bottle in one swallow. We sat on a bench and rested for a few minutes without speaking.

"Not bad for a pup," Rachel nodded.

"A pup?" I stammered, as my breathing was heavy.

"Newbie," she said. "I call new guys a pup."

"Wanna go get something to eat?" I asked.

"Are you serious?" She gaped at me. "You're asking me out?"

"No," I rolled my eyes. "I'm hungry."

"Hmm," she murmured.

"If I wanted to ask you out, I would've asked you out," I spat. "I'm hungry, you're here, so I
figured, what the hell, why not?"

"Well, I wouldn't go," she replied. "If you had asked me."

"You hungry? I don't have time for games," I sighed.

"Sorry," she growled.

I nodded. "So, what's next?"

"We'll work out some," she replied and cocked her

head. "Here comes Johnny." I turned my head to

see my uncle coming towards us.

"How'd it go?" He was looking at Rachel.

"Not bad for a pup," she said.

Johnny smirked. "A pup. Geez, Rachel, really?"

"Yeah, he's a pup, just learning his way. Someday he'll be a fighter."

"Hey, I got in a few good ones. What the " I exclaimed.

"A few won't win you a fight," Rachel growled. "A few won't even

get you into a cage more than once."

I glared at Rachel but didn't say a word. I knew she was right. Just

because I got a few blows in doesn't mean I'm ready to compete.

She's been fighting for years and knew what it took to get in the cage and win. She knew how to fight to win.

I nodded and stood.

"Johnny, can I talk to you for a minute?"

"All I have is a minute," he glanced at his wristwatch. "Make it quick."

We strode across the gym and went into his office. He stood in front of his desk with his arms crossed over his chest. "I hope this isn't about Rachel."

"No, nothing like that." I shook my head. "You know any cheap places around for me to stay? I only have a few hundred dollars and need a place to crash."

He inhaled deeply and released his breath. Shaking his head, he glanced out the window from his office in the gym.

"I don't know anyone out there looking for a roommate," he replied. "The only place I can think of is that rundown motel just outside town, east of the main drag."

"Yeah, been there," I replied. "No vacancy unless I wanna double up with some druggie. And I'm not going down that road."

"Stay here until you can find a place," Johnny replied. He strode across the office, opened a door I assumed was a closet, and flipped the overhead light on. "Not much, but it has a bed, table, chair, and mini-fridge. It's where I slept last night."

"Oh, hell, Johnny," I ran a hand through my hair. "I don't wanna put you out."

"Nah," he shook his head. "I was planning on heading home tonight. Not gonna let Marie rule the house that I pay for."

"If you're sure," I added.

"What's mine is yours, Jack," he nodded. "We may not be blood, but we're family." "Till the day we " I held up my fist, and he bumped it.

"I'll go grab my bag and stuff from my car," I said, turning to leave the office.

"Now don't go bringing no hoe back here," Johnny laughed, slapped me on the back, and we walked out.

***

Later that night, I came out of the backroom and saw some fighters

talking. I strolled over to them and listened to them for a few minutes.

"Hey," the dark-haired guy from earlier that was the first spectator

of Rachel and my fight. "We're heading to the Blue Thunder.

Wanna head out?"

"Sure," I replied, not knowing what the Blue Thunder was, but I

needed to get to know these guys. "Got nothing else going on."

"Liam," he held out a hand to me.

"Jack," I shook his hand.

Three other guys were hanging out. We introduced ourselves and then

left the gym. I headed to my car, and the other guys went to another

vehicle. I pulled up behind them and followed them to the Blue Thunder,

which turned out to be a local bar around the corner.

We all walked in together, and I saw Rachel sitting at the bar with

two other female fighters I recall seeing in passing at the gym. I

nodded to her and walked to the back, where Liam and the other

guys sat at a corner booth.

The Blue Thunder had a kitchen, so I ordered a deluxe burger with

a beer on tap. After the waitress brought the beers for everyone and my burger, Liam started in on me. "Man, one day soon, you

won't be eating that shit," Liam yelled over the loud music and

other people in the bar. "That one burger is all your calories for the

next few days."

"Yeah, I know," I smiled. "I figured this'll be my last meal."

"You know it," Liam slapped my back. "Especially with Queen

Rachel overseeing your training." "Huh? Why's that?" I'm intrigued

by the way Liam labeled Rachel a *queen.*

"What?" Liam took a swig of his beer. "Rachel, the queen?"

"Yeah," I said, taking the first bite of my burger. "Oh, man," I groaned

at how good and messy the burger tasted.

"She thinks she's all that," Liam leaned forward, his eyes

on Rachel across the room. "Why?" I took another bite of

the burger.

"You know any other word?" Liam tore his eyes away

from Rachel and glared at me. I shrugged and wiped my

mouth. "So, you gonna tell me?"

"Yeah," he drank more beer. "Just because she won a championship, she thinks she is better than the rest of us lowly cretins."

"I didn't get that," I said, taking the last bite of my burger. "She seems alright to me." "Watch your back with her," Liam warned, turning his scowl back in Rachel's direction. I didn't know what he meant by that, but I chose not to ask. It sounds as if there's bad blood between them, and I didn't want to be in the middle of that crap.

Chapter 4

Rachel

I spotted Jack, Liam, and some other guys from the Rogue Warrior as soon as they entered the Blue Thunder. I'm sitting at the bar, but with the mirror behind the counter, I can see the door in my view. Whenever someone walked in, the bright outdoor sunlight drew my attention.

I kept my eye on Liam as the guys passed by behind me. He glowered at me, and I rolled my eyes at him.

Liam and I have a past. Not a good one either.

It started on a whirlwind and ended in a disaster. Johnny almost kicked us both out of the gym because of the way our relationship ended. I'll be the first to admit I was unreasonable and purposely started the fights with Liam. But when he became obsessed with where I was, who I was with, and always seemed to be at every turn I made.

It got to a point where I finally went to Johnny, asking if Liam could have a different training and workout schedule than me. Johnny said he'd keep an eye on Liam, and if any funny business happened, he would confront Liam. I wasn't thrilled with it, but Johnny was the owner, and I held him to his word. One time, late in the evening, I was finishing my workout when Liam strolled over and began

Making accusations that I was carrying on with another fighter. Johnny overheard the exchange and told Liam to leave me alone or find another gym. Liam was spitting mad, slammed around the gym, threatened Johnny and me, then left. I thought that was the end of Liam bothering me or being at the

Rogue Warrior, but two weeks later, Liam reappeared, apologized to Johnny, and promised to keep his distance from me. Liam caused trouble wherever he disappeared to and was tossed out. Then he came back to Johnny cause word got out about him and his temper.

I turned my attention to Jack, who was eating a hamburger, sitting next to Liam, and every so often, his eyes traveled to me. My thoughts went to when Jack asked me to grab something to eat earlier. *Was it just a simple invite? Or had he been asking me out?* I didn't know for sure, but I would not get involved with another fighter. Especially one at the Rogue Warrior. Ever since that issue with Liam, Johnny's been strict about relationships.

Liam kept glaring at me from across the room, and I refused to glance away when we made eye contact. I'm not a person to stand down. I held his gaze, and I could tell Liam was agitated. I knew somehow, and some way, I was the source of his irritation. But I also felt Liam making 'friends' with Jack added to his annoyance, which was probably why he was surlier and grimmer than usual. Liam had asked me out one late night just before my championship fight. I had been training relentlessly and was high-strung on adrenaline for the upcoming match, and Liam had been so charismatic and attentive. He was there when I had to make weight. He supported me when I felt I couldn't go on. He was everything I wanted him to be.

But the day before my fight, Liam flipped. His personality and mannerisms went from encouraging and caring to over-protective and borderline possessive. I told him to tone it down, or he could get the hell away. He promised he didn't mean anything negative by his behavior. He claimed he was ensuring I could focus on the fight and didn't want anyone interfering with my training.

At first, I was skeptical, but Liam calmed down and became less confrontational with other people, and I accepted his reasoning. But after I won the championship fight, Liam attacked a reporter because the guy got too close to me during a post-fight interview. That's when I lost it. I told Liam to stay away from me, or I'd kick his ass. He knew I could do it, and I would if he pushed me. He became sour and vindictive, and any time I would talk to a male fighter, or any man for that matter, Liam would intimidate the guy. It was crazy, and I was not having any of it. I went to Johnny, explained the situation, and that's when the *hammer* came down. Johnny booted Liam from the gym and made it a new policy regarding relationships around the gym.

Quite a few fighters were pissed at me, and some even resented Liam, but since I was still at the gym and considered a favorite of Johnny's. I took the brunt of the disparaging comments and pissed-off glares. By the time Liam traipsed back to the gym weeks later, the other fighters' initial anger had gone away, and Liam was welcomed back into the fold.

That pissed me off. I took all the arguments and had to explain the situation, and was considered the bitch, and Liam was hailed the victim. I don't get how that crap works, but I've moved past it, as have most of the fighters. Liam still had his little group of guys who resented me, and I couldn't care less. I wasn't here to make friends or have a relationship. I was here to fight, be a better fighter, and work hard.

I should've known better than to get involved with Liam, but *damn*, I needed the distraction at the time and had all that extra energy to use up. It was a good release at the time, but I'll never do that again. I'd rather be known as the ice queen than have another tumble in bed with someone like Liam.

After I got to know him, I saw how controlling he was, how arrogant his personality was, and how possessive he could be.

I watched Jack finish his burger and chat with Liam. When Jack would glance in my direction, I was positive Liam had been filling him in with his version and not the truth.

"Don't let him get to you," Bree Anderson, another female fighter and probably my closest ally and friend at the gym, nudged my arm. "He's ruining your night."

"He's an asshole," I replied, picking up my glass and drinking ice water.
I wasn't a drinker and only came to the Blue Thunder with the girls once a week. It was a relaxing time, and I liked the camaraderie with the other woman fighters. They were a no-nonsense group, and I allowed myself this one evening to unwind, have some laughs, and act like a normal person.

Being an MMA fighter was anything but ordinary. Early mornings, long days of hard work, and a strict diet were what I signed up for. I knew that coming in, and it never detoured me. "Well, ladies," I stood. "I need to be heading home. Another long day tomorrow." "Oh, come on, Rachel," Bree yelled. "Don't let him dictate your life."

"He's' not," I replied. "I have Jiujitsu tomorrow morning after my warm-up. I'm feeling tired, so..." I waved a hand at my friends. "See y'all in the morning."

Groans from Bree and another girl sounded out as the other two women nodded. I tossed a few dollars on the table, and even though I only drank water, I left it mainly for the waitress' tip. I may be cheap, but I knew how working for a living wage could be.

I strode to the door and slipped out. The night sky was clear and a little cool, so I wrapped my arms around my midsection and got into my truck. I drove back to my loft and parked the truck. I felt more tired than when I left the bar a few minutes ago. I needed a good night's sleep and had to set aside the Jack and Liam scenario. If I didn't, I doubt I'd sleep at all tonight.

Chapter 5

I walked out of the animal shelter where I volunteered two days a week and climbed into my truck. I laid my forehead against the steering wheel. Days like today wore me out. Seeing all those Lovable dogs and cats just wanting to be petted, talked to or played with. It tore at my heart. I wish I could take them all home, but knew that wasn't possible.

I always promised myself that when I made it big, I'd go to this shelter and adopt every single animal they had inside. But that hadn't come yet, so I spent two half days here refilling water and food dishes, taking dogs out back in the fenced in area and tossing a ball around, or just petting the cats and talking to them.

As much as my emotions played on my heart seeing the sadness in the big brown eyes of the dogs, or the green eyes of some of the cats, I couldn't allow myself to grow too attached to them. They would either be adopted, or not there the next day. I set aside the reason for their disappearance and focused on the moment.

I started coming to this shelter soon after I settled into my fighter training and the apartment at Johnny's place. I had some free time one afternoon, and I was out jogging to clear my head when I ran past the shelter. I saw a volunteer in the fenced-in area playing with two medium-sized dogs. I stopped and spoke with the volunteer. The next day I went back to sign up, and ever since, I spent about ten to twelve hours a week there.

Despite the sadness of animals not being adopted, sad and passing on, the joy the dogs and cats brought me was worth it. Ever since I was a little girl, I had wanted a dog, but like most kids who lived like I did, that wish never came true. So, I guess being with these animals now was my way of fulfilling that dream.

I turned the key in the ignition, and the truck rumbled to life. I backed out of the parking lot and drove to the little grocery store near the Rogue Warrior. I needed to buy some groceries for the next week or two, and this was the only chance I'd have for a few days.

I pulled in front of the store and went inside. Grabbed a basket, and headed straight for the produce department. I picked out some sweet potatoes, bananas and other fruits and vegetables before heading to grab two jars of peanut butter, rice cakes and a variety of nuts and

seeds. By the time I

Headed to the cashier. My little grocery cart was full. I paid and took

the bags out to my truck. As I drove the short distance to the Rogue

Warrior, I ran through the next few days of my training, and Jack's

coaching. I had a pretty full schedule and needed to get home so I

could do some food prep for the week. If I had the food ready to go, it

made it easier for me.

I pulled into the gym's parking lot and steered my truck to near the

steps leading up to my apartment. I grabbed the three bags of food and

headed up the stairs. I was fumbling with the nags and trying to get

my keys out when I glanced up the stairs and saw Liam leaning

against the wall.

I groaned, as I didn't want to see him, let alone talk to him. "What do

you want, Liam?" I asked as I stuck my key in the lock.

"What's up with you and that Jack kid?" Liam cocked his head.

"What's it to you?" I opened the door, set my bags inside the

apartment. I turned back to Liam and saw him glaring at the parking

lot. I glanced over my shoulder and saw his eyes were fixated on

Jack's sedan.

"Have a problem with his car, too?" I smirked.

"Dammit, Rachel," Liam growled. "What's going on with you two?"

"Why does it matter to you?" I glared at him. "We are not a couple anymore, Liam." I crossed my arms over my chest.

"I don't like the kid," Liam sneered.

"I don't care," I said, reaching for the doorknob to go inside. "I have things to do." Liam's hand snapped out and grabbed my forearm. I pulled my arm, but his grip was too firm, and my arm was stuck in his hand. He squeezed his fingers, tightening his grip, and I winced. "Let me go, Liam," I warned. "You don't want to piss me off."

Our eyes locked, and I could see his hazel eyes full of anger. When Liam was mad, his eyes appeared greener than brown, and right now they were a dark emerald in color. His temper was bad, and I needed to diffuse it before he exploded. Luckily, he let my arm go.

"Liam, I really have a lot to do before my training later. Are we done?" I said, rubbing my forearm where he had his grip.

"Why won't you tell me?"

"About Jack?" I shook my head. "'Cause there's nothing to tell. I'm doing Johnny a favor by training him. Jack's his nephew. That's it. End of story."

Liam glowered at me, like he didn't fully believe my explanation.

"I don't know what else you want to hear, Liam," I replied, and shrugged. "I'm training him." "Well, I think the kid has a thing for you," Liam said.

"That's a joke," I laughed. "The kid's too green. He probably doesn't know what to do with a woman if he had a chance."

"Does he have a chance?" Liam hissed.

"With me?" I snorted. "Not likely."

"Better not," he growled. He stepped closer to me. "You're too good for him." I didn't like Liam being this close to me, and I stepped back. We didn't end on good terms, and having him within my space unnerved me.

"Step back, Liam," I stated. "You're not even supposed to be up here. If Johnny knew..." "Whatcha gonna do, Rachel? Go tattle on me?" Liam became angry.

"No, Liam," I stood my ground and stepped closer to him.

"I'll kick your ass, then get a restraining order. And you

know if I do that, you'll be out of the Rogue."

It's an idle threat, but Liam didn't know that.

"For fuck's sake, Rachel," Liam exclaimed. "I'm just trying to protect you."

"I don't need or want your protection," I replied.

"Don't mess with that kid," Liam warned.

"Or what? What's gonna happen?" I challenged.

"You don't want to know," Liam said, and moved towards the stairs.

"Mean it, Rachel, don't get involved with Jack."

"I heard you every time you said it," I replied. I opened my apartment

door and stepped inside. I closed the screen to keep a barrier between

Liam and myself. I watched him go down the stairs. He stopped after

four or five steps and yelled out.

"He's too young for you," and he cackled.

"Kiss my ass, asshole," I hollered back, and slammed the wood door.

I picked up my grocery bags, stalked to the kitchen and began unpacking the food. I slammed the sweet potatoes onto the counter and screamed.

"Damn you, Liam," I yelled.

Why did I always allow Liam to get under my skin? I didn't care what he thought, and he was not part of my life. I didn't understand why Liam was worried about Jack, or me becoming involved with Jack, aside from his jealousy and controlling personality.

First off, I'm an adult and can make my own decisions, whether good or bad. Second, Jack was not someone I would ever date, consider dating or sleep with. Jack's just not my type. *Right?* Jack's not someone I would date.

Was I trying to convince myself now?

I shook my head, grumbled and cussed, then started prepping my food for the rest of the week. I had to get Liam out of my head. But no sooner did I stop cursing him, my thoughts went to Jack. Jack had a lean body, and his muscles were developing at a good pace. While we'd only been working out a few days to this point, I noticed a lot of potential in Jack. When I first met him, and began training him, I admitted I wasn't fond of him, but over the last couple of days, I found him kind of intriguing. He was young, just starting in the MMA world of fighting, very impressionable, and I knew he'd be somebody someday.

I packed up the food, and had about two hours before my training with Josh at the Rogue, so I figured I'd lay on the sofa, shut my eyes for a few minutes and get my second wind. Seeing Liam earlier drained me for some reason. If I was going to get through my session and workout, having a few minutes to rest my eyes sounded perfect.

I settled onto the sofa, covered up with a blanket from the back of the sofa, and set my cell phone alarm for forty-five minutes, just in case I fell asleep. I closed my eyes, and my mind drifted back to Jack.

I was late for Jack's workout, and when I whipped open my apartment door, he was standing there. I opened my mouth to speak, but Jack placed his hand behind my neck and pulled my body to him. His mouth captured my lips, and my lips parted.

"Jack, we shouldn't do this," I mumble against his mouth.

"You know you want it though," he murmurs, and pulls my body harder toward him. "I do," I whispered. I felt my body tingle as

Jack's hands slipped under my tee-shirt and his fingers found their way to my breasts. I moaned when his fingers tweaked my nipples. "You like that, huh?" he whispers into my ear.

"Yes." I wrapped my arms around his neck and lulled my head back. His lips caressed across my skin, and I gripped his hair in my fingers. "Take me to the sofa," I begged.

Jack scooped me into his arms, and he strode to the sofa, and laid me back. He undressed as I took off my shirt and shorts. I slid my thong over my hips, but Jack stopped me. He placed his hand on mine and slipped his fingers beneath the fabric and lowered the thin piece of material.

He lowered his head and kissed my mound. I laid my hands on the top of his head, guiding him down.

"Stop," he muttered.

"I want you to taste me," I pushed his head again.

"No," he replied, stood up and got dressed. "You have to go, now."

"What? What the fuck, Jack!" I jumped up.

"Oh, crap!" I exclaimed when my eyes flung open. *A dream! A mother effing dream!*

Seconds later, the alarm on my phone started going off. I slapped the phone, turned off the alarm and sat with my head in my hands. I sighed and cussed at myself.

"What the hell was that?" I stood, stretched, and grabbed my duffle bag, and pushed Jack as far away from my thoughts as possible.

I needed to get to my training, but I mainly needed to find out why I was dreaming about Jack. I didn't like the kid, as a person, but as a fighter. I could learn to respect him. Where the hell the dream came from was beyond me.

I couldn't let some weird dream curtail my training, or interfere with how I trained Jack. Johnny would never forgive me for that.

<u>Chapter 6</u>

My face flew sideways, and my body crumbled to the mat. On all

fours, I hung my head low and spit out my mouthpiece.

"What the fuck was that? " I roared. "That's not cool!"

"Pay attention," Rachel hollered.

"You fuckin' hit me from behind," I growled. "You

fuckin' sucker punched me." "Gotta be ready at all

times," she shrugged, and took out her mouthpiece.

"You do that shit in the cage on fight night. You'd be pulled out," I

screamed. "You're a fuckin' bitch! What the hell did I do to you?"

 Rachel strode to the rope, grabbed a towel, and wiped her face off.
                                                    She climbed under the rope,
exiting the ring.

"Did you see that shit?" I complained to whoever was watching or

listening. "Can't take me down today, so you gotta do that illegal

shit!"

"Dude, she's hot on you," Liam replied from the other side of the
cage.

"She's a freakin' psycho," I yelled, and I knew she heard because she held up her hand and flipped the middle finger.

Liam laughed and walked closer to me. "I told you to watch your back with her, didn't I?" "Yeah, you did." I remembered the night at the Blue Thunder Bar. "I didn't think you meant it literally."

"She's bust your balls,' Liam sneered, glancing in Rachel's direction.

"Yeah," I wiped my face with a towel, and gathered up my bag and gear.

"Wanna go grab lunch?" Liam asked.

"Love to, but I'm officially training now," I replied.

"Ah, yeah," Liam nodded. "That sucks."

"You not training?" I asked.

"Not this year," Liam said. "Taking the year off from fights."

"Why's that?" I opened a water bottle and drank half of it in one swallow.

"Just taking the year to chill a little," he replied. "Things get so intense that I needed a break." I nodded, not fully understanding what he meant, but I figured I'd soon find out. I saw Johnny head into his office, and I told Liam I needed to go. I strode to my uncle's office, knocking on the door. "Come in," he yelled.

"Hey, got a minute?"

"Yeah, whatcha need?" Johnny shuffled through some papers on his desk.

"I got a situation with Rachel," I stated. I dropped my towel on the sofa near the door. "Dammit, Jack," Johnny threw papers down on his desk. "I told you," he pointed a finger at me, "that if you had a problem with her being a girl, then that's it!"

"No," I held up my hands. "It's not that."

"Then what?" he went back to searching through papers.

"She's being a psycho bitch," I exclaimed.

"Maybe she's PMSing," Johnny laughed.

"No," I shook my head. "She sucker punched me from behind. This wasn't a hormone thing." Johnny stopped sifting through the papers and glanced at me. "Sucker punched?" "Yeah." I stepped closer to his desk. "I was down, got up and turned around to get centered again, and *POW*," I jabbed my fist forward, "Right in the kidney!"

"I'll talk to " Johnny ran a hand through his hair and scratched.

"Johnny..."

"I said I'll handle it," he hissed.

"Fine," I shook my head, and grabbed my towel off the sofa. "Then handle it." "Hey!" Johnny erupted. "Get your ass back in here, NOW!"

I stopped, dropped my head and turned around.

"Don't you ever disrespect me like that again, you hear?" He circled his desk and stood a few feet from me. "Got it?"

"Yeah, I got it," I mumbled, my fingers twisting the towel in my hand.

"If you can't take a sucker punch every once in a while, when you're in the cage, then get the hell out," he yelled. "No one's keeping you here."

"Okay, I got it," I seethed. "But there's no reason for what she did. We were training, and all of a sudden, she fuckin' punched my back."

"I said I'd talk to her, and I will." Johnny's temper seemed to dissipate. "I don't condone that shit, and I'll talk to her."

"Thanks," I said and left the office.

I saw Rachel across the gym. Her eyes squinted as if she knew why I was in Johnny's office, but I didn't give a rat's ass. *Screw her*, I thought, and grabbed my duffle bag to head off to the showers. After I showered and change clothes, I decided to head out to the Blue Thunder. I'm sure I could catch up with Liam, or any of the other fighters there for the evening. I tossed my bag in the back storage room where I'd been living and walked out of the gym. The sun was going down and I figured a few light beers were in my future.

My adrenaline from the scene in the cage earlier was still raging, and I hope a few drinks and laughter with the other fighters would calm me down some. I decided to walk to the bar, and if I needed a ride home later, I'd hitch a ride with someone.

The evening air was cool and felt good as I walked. I thought about the scene with Rachel, and how she seemed too combative today, and then the bullshit from Johnny about talking to her. I doubted he'd talk to her. He just said that to pacify me, and that pissed me off, but I wasn't going to pursue it anymore. I had to pick my battles here, and I wasn't going to come off as some spinless wimp. I needed to stand up for myself, and I needed to pick my battles.

I opened the door and entered the bar. I saw Liam at the back table with a few other guys and waved to him. He saluted me with his beer bottle, and I went to the counter to get a beer. I ordered and waited for the barmaid to bring me a whatever was on tap that night, and I caught the eye of a bleach blonde girl at the bar. She smiled, I nodded to her, and she stood.

She approached me, and I guessed her to be just barely legal. She's in a bar, but that didn't mean she was of legal drinking age, but right now I couldn't care less. My blood was pumping, and I was full of energy. As she drew closer, I saw she was pretty, but not in a way that had men taking a second glance, but she had a trim body, firm figure and full breasts.

She's wearing a short denim skirt, a camisole tank top, and no bra that I could detect, and I felt my heart pound and my cock stiffen. *Perhaps I had found a way to release my energy and adrenaline tonight.*

"Hey," she yelled over the music and noise of the people inside the bar. "You're new." "Yeah," I smiled, and noticed her big brown eyes, circled with way too much mascara and eye makeup. *But, hey, I wasn't going to worry about that.*

"You with them." She cocked her head to the back table where Liam was sitting. "Yeah," I watched the guys laughing at the table, but decided I could probably blow off more steam with her than them.

"You at the Rogue, too?"

"Yeah, Johnny's my uncle," I answered as the barmaid slid my glass in front of me. I slipped a twenty out of my pocket and nodded for two more beers. One more for me, and one for my new friend.

"Mmmmm," she murmured.

The barmaid brought over the two beers, and I grabbed two of the beers, and went to a table in the opposite corner of where Liam was at, and held out a chair for the blonde. She brought the third beer. "What's your name?" She asked as she sat.

"Jack," I replied. "And you?"

"Jenna," she smiled and sipped her beer.

"Pleasure to meet you, Jenna," I said, and straddled the chair.

We sat and talked, but I only heard every other, or third, word she said, as the Blue Thunder was busier than normal. It being a Friday night; I assumed. We had another beer each, when Jenna leaned into me, placed her hand on my crotch, and smiled.

"You wanna get out of here?"

"Fuckin' A," I yelled. "Let's go."

We stood. I waved to Liam, who saluted me again with his beer, and I escorted Jenna out of the bar. Once outside, and when my ears stopped vibrating from all the noise inside, Jenna grabbed my hand and we walked to a little two-door sports car. She opened the drivers' door and slid in, so I circled the car and climbed into the passenger seat.

"Let's go," she purred, and started the engine. "I need a good fucking."

"Yeah," I reached across the front seat, grabbed behind her neck and pulled her face to mine, kissing her. "Me too."

She put the car in reverse and backed out. Then she pulled out of the parking lot, and turned in the opposite direction of the Rogue, and sped down the street. I slipped my left hand under her skirt and moved aside her panties, and found her moist.

"Damn," I growled, as my fingers spread her folds apart and two fingers plunged into her wetness. "Oh, fuck," she moaned and pulled into an apartment complex. "We'll be inside my place in a minute. Hang on."

She parked the car, and we both got out and ran to the door. She fumbled with her keys to unlock the door, as I kissed her again, and fondled her breasts. I leaned against her, and she hit the door, causing it to open. We fell on the floor, and I picked her up and slammed the door with my foot.

I carried her to the sofa and didn't even bother stripping down. I hiked up her skirt, pulled her soaked panties off her body and I dropped my jeans to my ankles. I mounted her and she moaned as I entered her.

"Faster." she gripped my shoulders as I plunged deeper.

I rode her hard and felt the stress of the events earlier lifting off me. With my final plunge into her, I thought of Rachel, and exploded.

"Oh my God," she moaned as her hips stopped moving. "That was incredible." "Yeah," was all I could say. I collapsed onto her, and eventually climbed off her and sat on the floor with my back against the sofa. Her fingers were stroking my back, and every so often she'd hit a spot and my body would flinch. Not because I didn't want Jenna touching me, but I kept imagining it was Rachel who I just had sex with.

Rachel's face kept popping into my head, and I could see her brown eyes staring back at me when I shut my eyes.

"Want something to drink?" Jenna asked, got up and walked to the little kitchen on the other side of the room. She straightened her denim skirt and adjusted her tank top that got all twisted. "Yeah, sure," I replied, grabbing my jeans to slip back into. "You live here alone?" "I do," she said, and handed me a beer. She set hers down on a table beside the sofa and sat on the sofa. "I had a roommate, but she was kinda weird. I asked her to move out a few months ago." I sat on the sofa beside her, drinking my beer. "I'll stay the night," I said.

"Damn straight you are," Jenna laughed, picked up her beer and drank.

I drained my beer and stood. "Let's go to bed. I've had a horrible day."

"Until you met me, that is," she giggled.

"Yeah," I replied and followed her to the bedroom.

<u>Chapter 7</u>

I'm wrapping my fingers, preparing to enter the cage for training, when two male fighters stroll past, laughing. Normally, I ignore the gossip around the gym, but when I hear Jack's name mentioned, my ears perk up and eavesdrop. I slowed down the tape wrapping to linger and listen in.

The guys, Trevor and Ian, were experienced fighters, and if I remember correctly, Ian is a middleweight, and Trevor is a light heavyweight. They're both highly skilled men and had the wins to back up the facts. I've never really mingled with them, but in a tight fighting community, you knew who was who, and who was a friend, and who was not.

I didn't have any riff with these guys, and I'd seen them heading out last night, probably for the Blue Thunder. I also knew Jack had left the gym in a pissed off mood, thanks to me, and he more than likely made his way there, too. I was too drained to be good company, so I stayed home, relaxed and let my body and mind rest.

I wasn't the social butterfly that most female fighters were, and I liked it that way. Being an introvert had its advantages. No one bothered you, as they thought you were brooding and standoffish. They didn't strike up a conversation because you really didn't contribute to the chatter. "So, did he stay the night?" Trevor asked Ian.

"As far as I know he did," Ian replied, and began unpacking his gym bag.

"You think maybe one of us should have told him?"

"About Jenna?" Ian chuckled. "And said what, exactly?"

"I don't know," Trevor shrugged, dropping his bag on the floor.

"Maybe that she's just a groupie." "Who's looking for some strange?" Ian laughed. "Hell, every one of us needs a girl like that." I tensed when I imagined Jack spending the night with this Jenna. I think I knew who she was, but couldn't be sure. If I'm not mistaken, she's a bleach blonde who's on the shorter side and has a reputation of hanging out at the Blue Thunder, and, on the occasion, at the gym, depending on who she's banging that week.

The fingers on my left hand tightened their grip on the tape, and when

I felt two of my fingers on my right-hand tingling, I loosened the tape. On a normal day, I would have had both hands taped and been in the cage already and loosening up, but I felt an undeniable urge to continue listening to Trevor and Ian. Mindlessly listening to the conversation, I kept wrapping my fingers, and at this rate, I'd use an entire roll of sticky tape before I heard the entire story.

"I think we've all had *that* girl," Trevor laughed. "I know I did."

"Yup," Ian nodded. "But that kid's been stowing up more frustration than any of us." "Not likely," Trevor cocked his head. "We've all had the training."

"Not the training," Ian shook his head. "But the *trainer.*" Trevor nodded, then turned to say something else, but his eyes made contact with me, and he swore.

"Fuck, Rachel," he muttered, which caused Ian to spin around.

"Hey, sorry, Rachel," Ian hung his head.

"Yeah," I spat, ripped the end of the tape and slammed the roll on the bench, and stood. "Fuck off all of you!"

I stormed off to the cage and climbed inside. I knew I'd be in rare form today, and I also knew I'd be extra harsh on Jack. *Screw all that shit* about training him. I was out for vengeance now. I was tired of being the topic of all the gossip around here. I was growing weary of the guys, thinking I was nothing but the *ice queen*. I did nothing to Trevor *or* Ian. They're basing all their laughs and ridicule of me from the lies Liam told. As of today, I'm done with that.

I vowed the next time Liam started his crap; I was going to blow. I'd set the record straight to whomever was there, and make sure *everyone* knew what a jerk, and liar, he was. I don't usually care what people think of me, but hearing Trevor and Ian with their locker room talk about Jack and this Jenna, sent me reeling.

I don't know why it bothers me so much, but *damn it*, I was fuming.

***

"Mother effer!" Jack roared.: "What the hell's wrong with you?"

He stepped away from me and spit his mouth guard into his gloved hand. "This shit is getting old!"

I shrugged, spitting out my mouth guard. "And I told you, if you can't fuckin' handle it, then you're not made for this."

Jack narrowed his eyes, his chest puffing in and out, and I saw his hands bawling up in fists, then releasing. His frustration with me was evident, but I didn't give a shit.

"You need to get your anger under control," Jack pointed a finger in my face. "I'm not your freaking whipping boy!"

I shrugged and glanced away from Jack. I knew he was right in his accusation, but I'm not going to own up to it for him.

"I don't know what shit you're pissed about, but you need to get over it," Jack glared at me, and walked to the corner of the cage. He picked up a water bottle and drained the entire bottle. "Now let's go again," he said, and came back to the middle of the cage. He held up his hands, waiting for me to take my stance.

I sighed, put my mouth guard back in my mouth, and waited for Jack to begin his circling. He's so predictable, and within a second, he was moving to his right.

I followed, allowing him to lead. He took a left jab, then

immediately thrust his right hand forward. I blocked the move, knowing it was coming before he tried to strike.

"Come on," I yelled. "You use the same delivery *every time*! Mix it up!"

"Old habits," Jack yelled.

"Change your ways then," I dared him. "You'll never break the habit if you don't try something new."

"Yeah, I'm sure you know *all about* that!" He roared, jabbing with his left hand, then kicked up and hit me right in the side of my abdomen.

If he had been more centered, he would've hit me square on target, and could've taken me down in a split second. *I was impressed.*

"What's that mean?" I stopped to catch my breath after his kick.

"Forget it," he said, and spun around, then thrust his right hand to the side of my head. I was still focusing on his statement, and its meaning, that his strike caught me off-guard. The blow to my head made my head snap, and I stumbled to the rope to gain my composure. "What the fuck does that mean!!" I glowered.

Jack shook his head. "You're a smart girl. Figure it out."

"Damn it, Jack!" I seethed. "I don't have time for this childish shit."

"And I don't have time for your bullshit either," he said, removing

his mouth guard. He moved away, climbed out of the cage, and

glanced back at me. "When you're over whatever hormonal crap

you're dealing with and are ready to train me, you know where to

find me."

Jack glared at me, and I couldn't hold back. "What did

you mean by that little jab?" "Oh, come on, Rachel,"

his head flopped back. "Are you serious?"

"Yeah, you started it, so finish it." I had my fists balled on my hips.

"Fuck, Rachel," he shook his head. He walked to where I stood.

He leaned in close and whispered, "I know all about how you

screw with guys. I know how you use them. It may not be a habit,

but it's disgusting. Change *your ways.*"

"You don't know what the fuck you're talking about," I hissed.

"You're falling for all the bullshit and gossip."

"Maybe, maybe not," he shrugged, then turned to walk away.

"Either way, you sure make the perception easy to believe."

"Go to hell," I roared, walked away and climbed out of the cage.

I grabbed my towel, water bottle and bag, then bolted out of the gym. I sprinted across the parking lot, climbed the stairs to my apartment two at a time, and crashed inside. I slammed my apartment door shut and threw my bag across the small room.

"Mother effing!" I screamed once I was alone.

I collapsed onto the worn-out sofa in the living room and laid the back of my hand on my forehead. *So, Jack believed all the bullshit that Liam, and who knows who else, was spewing about me.* I shouldn't care, but damn it, coming from Jack, it really bothered me. Either he was too shallow and believed everything, or I *was really* that girl. I preferred to believe Jack had a superficial personality and would be gaslighted, but I began thinking about Liam, and how Our relationship developed, and his jealousy. I know when it came to Liam; I was in the right. No one should have to deal with an over-possessive person, but I began wondering if I had fed into his controlling personality and led him to be that way.

"Hell, no!" I roared. His decision making and clingy behavior was already established. I had nothing to do with that.

So I went back deeper into previous relationships, trying to find other ways I could have encouraged men, then dropped them like a hot potato. I couldn't find any, and knew all my relationships had ended either mutually, or in some dire circumstances.

"Screw him," I groaned.

I couldn't let what Jack said, or implied, affect me. I wouldn't allow his words to distract me. *Easier said than done.* I wiped a tear away as it fell on my cheek.

"Why the hell are you so emotional?" I cried. "Let it go. Jack means nothing, right?" I couldn't honestly answer that. I wanted to believe it, but *damn*, when I saw Jack, my stomach flopped, and I felt a sexual drive I hadn't felt in forever. I'd been so focused on my career and getting back on top of my weight category.

But then Jack showed up in my world, and I didn't know how to handle his appearance. First, I was upset about him being here and I had to train him, then I was pissed because he threw me off kilter. Now I'm furious because he has such a low view and impression of me.

"Oh, my God, Rachel," I groaned again. "Get him outta your freakin' head!"

Chapter 8

"Loverboy," Ian chuckled, and nodded towards the main gym door.

"You got company." I glanced over my shoulder from where me and

Ian were running through our shadowbox exercises. I was holding

the bag while he did his reps. My eyes narrowed in on Jenna

standing at the door, scanning around the gym, looking for me.

This is the third time in the last two days, since our meeting at the

Blue Thunder, that she'd come to the gym. I spent the first two nights

at her place, banging her and getting some pent-up frustrations out of

my system, but I wasn't looking for some forlorn girl hovering my

every second. She's becoming a nuisance that I no longer wanted

around.

But damn, she's wild in bed. While that trait shouldn't run my life,

right now I needed the distraction of her warm body and salacious

sexual inhibitions. When she howled as she came, it sent my body

into a frenzy of release. It didn't matter, as she called out my name, that I was envisioning Rachel beneath my body, accepting every thrust as I drove deeper and deeper.

"What the fuck," I sighed.

"Better go talk to her," Ian said. "You can only avoid chicks like her for so long." "Yeah, I suppose," I released the punching bag, and strode to where Jenna was standing. As soon as she saw me, she smiled and began walking in my direction. I really wasn't in the mood

To chat, or even see her, but I knew if I didn't, she'd keep coming back, or track me down at the bar. "Hey," she fluttered her eyelashes, and widened her smile. "You going to the Thunder tonight?" "Not sure," I answered vaguely. "Why?"

"Just curious." She replied. "I miss you."

"We were just together yesterday," I grumbled.
"I " she ran a finger on my forearm. "But a girl has needs."

I pulled my arm away from her and shrugged.

"You don't seem so interested," she pouted.

"I'm busy, Jenna," I mumbled. "Anything else?"

"No," her pout deepened. "Jack, I just... I *really*

enjoy our time together, is all." "Yeah, so do I," I

replied. "But you can't keep coming in here."

"Why not?" she fluttered her eyelashes again.

"Fuck, Jenna," I mumbled. "I don't bother you when you're at work, or busy."

"I'll just sit and watch," she smiled. "You won't even know I'm here."

"Jenna," I rolled my eyes.

"Hey, Jack!" Ian called. "C'mon man."

"I gotta go," I said to her, and she nodded.

I strode back to Ian, who was holding the bag for me. I began doing my

reps, all the while knowing Jenna was sitting on a bench near a cage and

watching me. This threw me off, and I was fumbling with my jabs and

punches.

I was almost finished with my reps when I saw Rachel enter the gym.

She walked to the locker room, and *damn* if she didn't look sexier

than hell. Her hair pulled back in the usual ponytail, bouncing as she

walked, and her muscular body filled out her workout clothes. The

way her shorts hugged her hips, and the tight tank top clung to her

breasts, slammed into my chest.

"Damn it," I plowed my fist into the punching bag, catching Ian off balance.

"What the hell, dude!" Ian yelled.

"Sorry," I shrugged. "I had one bigger one in me."

"Showing off for your girl," he laughed, taking the tape off his fingers.

"No," I growled. "She's not my girl." I was saying this in relation to Rachel, not Jenna, but Ian didn't need to know this.

"Yeah, okay," Ian shrugged. "I'm heading off to shower. You coming?"

"No," I replied. "I want to do some more cooling off and reps."

"Okay," he said, and walked towards the locker room, and I glanced in Jenna's direction. She wasn't paying attention to me. She was sitting on the bench still, but talking to another fighter. From here, it seemed as if she was flirting with the guy, and I wasn't bothered by it at all. I had to admit, it was relief seeing her focusing her preoccupation on someone other than me. Sure, Jenna was a great lay, but I didn't see her as anything more.

I went to the corner, grabbed a rope, and began skipping with it. My eyes were glued to the locker room doors, waiting for Rachel to come out. I'd lost count of how many reps I've done when she emerged. She was fitting her gloves on over the tape she must've adhered in the locker room, and she strolled in the direction of where Jenna was still chatting with the other fighter.

Rachel approached the couple, and as soon as she spotted Jenna, a scowl developed on Rachel's face. The disdain for the other girl was more than obvious when Rachel rolled her eyes and steered away from the bleach blonde.

I glanced at Jenna, who glimpsed in my direction, and smirked, as if she was trying to get a *rise* out of me, but I let it roll off my shoulders. I had no intention of being jealous, not over Jenna, at least. I stopped jumping, and put the rope back on the wall peg, and headed to the locker room. I was done for the day, and since I didn't have practice or training with Rachel today, I decided to make it an early day.

The last time I trained with Rachel, we had our words, and I was still a little pissed about it. I didn't know how she felt and didn't care. She'd been *playing* a little dirty lately during our training, and I held my ground and put her in her place, which made me feel good.

I fought hard to not look back at Rachel as I entered the locker room, but was successful. I couldn't explain why Rachel got to me when I saw her, or how much I fantasized about her was insane. Rachel filled my every waking moment, and I couldn't stop envisioning her naked beneath me.

After showering, I headed to my room off the office. I saw Jenna still hanging around and shook my head at her determination. I tossed my dirty clothes in a cardboard box I was using as a laundry hamper and figured I'd have to wash everything soon. I only had two more workout outfits, and my room started having that odor most people referred to as a locker room stench.

As soon as I walked out to the gym, Jenna came over to me, looped her arm through mine, and we were off to her place. As I drove my car, she was all over me, and by the time we got to her apartment, my sexual frustration was high.

No sooner did she open her apartment door, we were stripping out of our clothes, and I was fast and furious. I couldn't wait to slip my erect shaft into her, and as soon as I was thrusting into her, my mind imagined it was Rachel calling out my name.

Chapter 9

Rachel

I kicked the bag out of my way and glared at the other female fighter, who had left it on the walkway between the lockers. I was in no mood for anyone or anything. My foul mood had been here for the last few days. Ever since Jenna showed up at the gym to ogle Jack, flirt with whatever fighter was nearby and to try to stare me down.

If Jenna thought I was intimidated by her, she was wrong. Girls like her were a dime a dozen, and I had no use for them. She's nothing more than an overzealous fan who'll sleep with, every fighter she thought could be the next prize fighter. She was in this for glory, and the easy fucks. She didn't care about the guys she slept with, she just wanted the fame and fortune that went along with it. I knew of at least five guys Jenna had carried on with in the last two years. Her track record was nothing to brag about. None of the guys she took to her bed ever amounted to anything. The five guys she had been with in this gym alone, one of them, were still here. I didn't know if they left the MM for good, or if they just moved on to another gym, but either

way, Jenna was a prowess, and I had no use for her. She was just a

distraction, and if someone was serious about making a name for

themselves in this sport, you needed to stay one-hundred percent

focused. I strode out to the gym and headed for the punching bag. I

had way too much energy and adrenaline that I needed to burn off.

Just yesterday, Jack confronted me about mind my own business. I had

told him to watch his back when it came to Jenna, and he went off. He

began ranting about how I was just jealous and that I needed to get

laid. He screamed it so loud, half the gym stopped and stared. The

silence was deafening, and my first instinct was to run off, but I knew

if I did that, then the entire gym would ride my ass about it. Which

was not the reputation I wanted.

So, instead of hightailing it out of there, I went off on him. We were in

a heated argument when Johnny came up, splitting us apart. He told

Jack to go shower, then he told me to go to his office. I was pissed that

Jack had gotten to me and struck a nerve, but I was more pissed that I

was going to be reprimanded by Johnny.

I slammed into Johnny's office and began pacing. I wasn't at fault for the display in the gym. I was just forewarning Jack to be careful

because he was the guy, I was training, and if he wasn't focusing on

fighting and our sessions, it would reflect badly on me.

"Before you say one word, I'm speaking first," Johnny slammed the

office door, and went to sit in his chair. "Have a seat."

"Johnny..." I began.
"Stop." he held up a hand. "This isn't about what happened out

there." He pointed to the gym. "It isn't?" I shook my head and sat

on the sofa.

"No," he said, leaning back in the chair and crossing his legs on the

desk. "I've been wanting to talk with you for a few days now, but

never found the time."

"" I narrowed my eyes.

"I just wanted to touch base and let you know what a frickin' fabulous

job you've been doing with Jack," Johnny smiled.

"Really?" I leaned back on the sofa, more relaxed.

"Fuck yeah," Johnny nodded. "That boy has developed a backbone,
finally."

"Yeah, don't I know?" I rolled my eyes. "He's been getting on my nerves with his bullshit." "I see that," Johnny chuckled.

"What the hell was that all about?"

"Just a warning for him to stay focused and not let some easy lay

cloud his judgement and skills," I shrugged.

"Yeah, I saw Jenna poking around the other day," he shook his head.

"Nothing but trouble in my mind."

"Sure is," I nodded, "And she's got her hooks in Jack."

"Poor kid," Johnny smirked. "Guess he'll learn a lesson."

"The hard way," I added.

"Not our problem," Johnny said.

"It's mine if he's too focused on getting laid instead of training," I
countered.

"True," Johnny nodded. "Want me to talk to him?"

"Fuck no," I grimaced. "You do that and he'll think I cried to you."

Johnny nodded, pushed off his chair, lowered his feet and stood. "I'll

leave it be, but if he gets too out of hand, let me know."

"Will do," I said, and stood.
"Also, your training may need to take a backseat for

a few more weeks," he said. "What! Why!" I fumed.

"Jack needs a little more attention," Johnny said. "He's on the right track, thanks to you, but he's not ready for the cage."

"What the hell, Johnny?" I cringed. "I've already given up weeks of my own training." "I know," he said. "But you're disciplined, and he's not. He needs to be run through the gamut." "Great." I threw my hands in the air. "I'll barely have enough time to prep for my own fights. I didn't sign on for this."

"I know," he said. "Just a favor, for a favor."

I sighed, knowing Johnny was right. He'd been letting me live rent free in the crappy little apartment for years, so this was the least I could do.

"Anything else?" I asked.

"Yeah, when's the last time you got laid? Maybe Jack's onto something," Johnny roared. "Shut the fuck up," I said, stormed out of the office, slamming the door in my wake.

Chapter 10

I strolled into the gym a few days after the scene with Rachel in the gym. I've been staying at Jenna's place, as I didn't want to be anywhere close to Rachel. The bitch was infuriating and could make me crazy just by seeing her. She was an excellent trainer, and I didn't want to cause too much of a problem to make her leave. As much as I was pissed about Johnny sticking me with her in the beginning, I was grateful he had. But I'd never tell Johnny or Rachel that.

Rachel was a hard-ass, and I knew when we had our sessions, I'd be exhausted that night. She expecting nothing but perfection, and thought nothing of me having to do rounds and reps repeatedly. She's aggressive, ruthless and adamant on getting everything right. I suppose that's partially why she's a champion, and so well-respected in the MMA world. She had a structured schedule and regime, worked herself to exhaustion and definitely deserved all the esteem from others.

But damn, that fucking woman could drive me crazy!

One second, I was hot and heavy for her, the next, she was ridiculing me and pushing me to my limits. I saw a few times the way she glimpsed at me. I knew that fire in a woman's eyes. Rachel left me feeling sexually aroused, and then she'd beat me down.

Thank God I had Jenna waiting for me, ready, willing and able. Any time I found myself hard, and in need of release, Jenna was there. She was a salacious woman in bed, and could pleasure me in more ways than I ever imagined I wanted. She was hardcore into sex, and she knew exactly what I needed, when I didn't even know.

Like the other day when I went to her place all pissed off about Rachel, and all Jenna did was get down on her knees, pull my shorts down and wrapped her luscious lips around my shaft and began sucking. I leaned against the door. Luckily, it had been there, and she brought out a climax that was much appreciated.

Sad thing is, the entire time Jenna had her lips wrapped around me, all I could see was Rachel, and that pissed me off more. Rachel's big brown eyes were staring up at me, not Jenna's blue eyes. It was Rachel's lips, and a hand was stroking my cock, not Jenna. It was Rachel that I wanted. "Ugh," my head fell back onto the door as I came.

Seconds later, Jenna stood, wiped her mouth and went into the

kitchen. "Rough day at the office?" She giggled.

"Yeah, I guess," I grunted as I pulled my shorts back up. "I'm

hungry. Whatcha got to eat?" "Not much," she said, opening

the small refrigerator. "Nope, nothing."

"Great," I mumbled, walking into the kitchenette area.

"Aren't you supposed to be on a special diet?" Jenna asked.

"Yeah," I grumbled, sifting through the refrigerator. "Damn it!" I

slammed the door and went to the apartment door.

"Where are you going? You just got here," Jenna whined.

"Out," I said and left the apartment.

"What the hell, Jack?" Jenna opened the door,

yelling at me. "You just got here!" I continued

walking, and held up a hand, flipping her my middle

finger.

"Asshole!" she screamed, then I heard the door slam.

I chuckled and went out to the parking lot. I jogged back to the gym and figured I'd take a shower, then go get something to eat.

"Screw the diet," I muttered as I got to the gym. "I need actual food."

I entered the gym and saw other fighters working out. Some were in the cages doing rounds, and a few more were standing around talking and laughing. I didn't see Rachel, and felt a little mad about that. My adrenaline was still running high, and I needed to get in the shower before I busted. I wished it were my time for training, because I sure could use some time to work off the aggression. I went to Johnny's office, and my room was in the back. I grabbed a towel and some clean clothes before heading off to the locker room for a shower.

I waved to Liam and a few other guys before pushing the door that lead to the hallway. As I was passing by the women's locker room, the door flung open and Rachel ran into me. "Whoa," I held up an arm to stop her from tripping.

"What the...?" she pulled away from me.

"Screw you," I growled, leering at her.

"Why are you such an ass?" she hissed.

"Me? I'm getting tired of your attitude," I spat. "All I ever do is work, train and take your shit!" "My shit?" She crossed her arms over her chest. "Attitude? You really are an asshole!" My adrenaline was already pumping after being at Jenna's, and thinking about Rachel, and now seeing her all pissed off and full of rage turned me on more than I could ever imagine. I acted on impulse, and be damned what repercussion came from it.

I grabbed Rachel by the shoulders, leaned her into the wall, and captured her lips with mine. At first she fidgeted, and tried to free her mouth, but after a few seconds, she gave in and wrapped her arms around my neck. Her lips parted, and my tongue slid across her lips. She moaned as my tongue slipped inside her mouth. Her hands moved to my hair, and she entwined her fingers.

My lips moved to her chin, and she tilted her head back, exposing her neck, and I began running my lips and tongue over her skin. She tasted as if she'd just gotten out of the shower and smelled like flowers. I felt a twinge in my groin, and soon my shaft was stiffening. I rubbed my hips against hers, and she groaned, pulling my head away from her neck. Her lips seized my mouth, and her tongue kept darting in and out of my lips.

"Oh, God," she moaned as her lips parted from mine. Her brown eyes sought my gaze, and I lowered my head to kiss her again, when suddenly she pushed me away, and hauled off and slugged me in the stomach.

"What the fuck, Jack!" she yelled.

As I buckled over, holding my abdomen from the punch, she stormed off down the hallway. I was panting, trying to catch my breath, when she yelled. "That's a sucker punch! In case you didn't know, asshole!"

She slammed out the door leading to the gym, and I leaned against the wall. Once I had regained my composure, I smirked.

"Yeah, that bitch wants me," I laughed, heading off to the men's locker room for a much-needed shower.

Chapter 11

Rachel

I slammed into my apartment and collapsed onto the sofa. Closing my eyes, I laid an arm on my forehead and envisioned what had just happened between me and Jack. How had I let it happen? Was the first thought I had? My second one was, why did I enjoy it so much?

I groaned, and continued laying there, thinking about how good his body felt against mine, and how I didn't want the kiss to end. But to save face, I had to sucker punch him. I didn't want to get involved with Jack, or any man, for that matter. Especially Jack.

He's Johnny's nephew, and Johnny had strict rules against staff and fighters in the gym getting sexually, or romantically, hooked up. Too much could happen, or go wrong with two people associated within the gym. I knew that all too well.

"Thanks to me," I sighed.

The entire Liam fiasco came to mind, but I brushed it aside. I didn't want to relive that total nightmare again, even in my head.

Ever since the problem, Liam and I kept our distance from one another. But I could feel the glares from him, and some of his buddies, in the gym. I ignored everything about Liam, and knowing Jack had sort of been taken in by Liam made the possibility of ever getting involved with Jack was not on my radar.

But damn, that kid could kiss!

Which brought me to another reason for avoiding any relationship with Jack, aside from being his trainer and a fellow fighter in the same gym, was how much older I was than him. But I guess thirteen years really isn't that big of a deal to some, but it was to me.

People really didn't frown upon when a man was older than a woman, but when it was a woman who was older, there was some backlash. Unless you were a super sexy lady, then you were considered a *cougar*.

But I was anything but a sexy lady. Even as a teenager, I was more of a tomboy, and didn't really get into the *girly-girl* scene. During my junior and high school years, when my classmates, and friends, would be getting their hair and nails done for prom or other events, I was known for throwing on a pair of dirty jeans, a sweatshirt and whatever shoes were nearby.

I just didn't care what I looked like, and couldn't care less about getting a date every Friday or Saturday night. I preferred to stay home, read or just hang out. Dating was a social happening I didn't partake in. And when I left home at seventeen, I wasn't around for my senior prom. But that was fine. I wouldn't have attended, anyway.

Liam was my first serious relationship, and the way that ended really turned me off from seeking a boyfriend. I was content with how my life was going and figured a guy would just mess things up. I pushed up and sat on the edge of the sofa, placing my elbows on my knees. I glimpsed around my apartment. While it was small, it was enough for me. Three rooms, if you included the bathroom, and I was hardly ever here. I spent most of my time in the gym, even preferring to use the shower stalls there instead of here. The other place I spent most of my time at was the animal shelter across town. This wasn't a place I'd bring a guy to, even if I had a boyfriend. The furniture, while sparse, had been here when I moved in, and the only pieces I'd added were bookshelves, that was loaded with books I got for free at the library sales, and a small outdoor table with two chairs that I used as a dining room table. I never actually ate there. It was more for a place to put my dirty clothes and other crap on when I came home.

I saw my headgear sitting in the middle of the table, and my thoughts went back to Jack. And that kiss. My heart rate had slowed down, and I was able to catch my breath before I climbed the steps to the apartment, but *damn*, I didn't want the kiss to end.

I began counting off the reasons not to get involved with Jack, but the thoughts of sleeping with him really came forefront to me. Granted, I had thought of the possibility over the last few weeks, ever since he arrived at the gym, but today my mind was being overtaken with images of me and him banging each other.

I would never admit to anyone how much seeing Jack every day turned me on, and how I had fantasies about him naked beneath me, or hovering over me. Over the last few weeks, I've had every possible scene play over in my head. I'd released my sexual desire for him more times than I cared to say. But after the pleasure, my libido grew more for him, and the way we kissed earlier really had me riled up.

I stood, headed to the bathroom, and stripped down. I turned on the shower and stepped under the water. It wasn't warm yet, but the cold

from the water helped ease my frustration. As the water began

changing temperature, I settled in for my shower. I was going to

shower at the gym, but I had forgotten my bag, and had to leave the

women's locker room to get it. That's when Jack stopped me.

After we kissed, my head was not comprehending what I had been

doing, or needed to do, so I left the gym to come back here to gather

my thoughts. I'd left my duffle bag on the gym bench, forgot bout the

shower and found myself in my apartment before I could set my mind

to what I was going to do.

I leaned against the shower tile, and let the water beat across my skin.

I laid my head back, and my hands went down between my legs. As

my fingers separated my folds, my mind thought of Jack doing

This. His fingers seeking my pleasure as I held the back of his head,

guiding him. Closing my eyes, I moaned as my fingers rubbed and

swirled, finding the nub of my passion. I rubbed harder, as I pictured

Jack's tongue in place of my fingers. I bit my lower lip as I prolonged

my climax. When I couldn't hold it in any longer, I let my release

come, groaning as my finger became wetter from the pinnacle of my coming.

The water sluiced over my skin, and I opened my eyes. I remained still for a minute to regain my composure. My legs were shaky, and I needed to brace myself against the tile until I was stable. Once I was able to stand, I turned off the water and stepped out of the shower stall. I grabbed a towel off the rack and dried my body off.

I slipped into an oversized tee-shirt and went into my small bedroom. Falling onto the bed, I laid there until my breathing returned to normal.

Chapter 12

Jack

"What the fuck!" my head bounced back, and I glared at Rachel.

"Stop being such an asshole!" "You need to be ready for whatever your opponent is gonna throw at you," she said, shifting from foot to foot. "You never know what's coming your way."

"I'm getting tired of your bullshit!" I yelled, taking my mouthpiece out. "You need to grow the fuck up!"

"Whatever." she waved a hand at me, which pissed me off more.

Her flippant attitude, and how she fought dirty, was getting on my last nerve.

Ever since we kissed a few days ago, she'd been working me harder in the cage, and I was exhausted. Our three hours a day together was turning into four, and yesterday, five hours. My body was revolting, and every muscle hurt at night. I'd even been slowing down when I went back to Jenna's place at night.

Jenna complained this morning when I turned down her advances. She came out of the bathroom naked, and four days ago, I would've jumped her, or let her ride my shaft until she begged me to stop. But this morning, I groaned when she strolled to the bed and straddled my hips.

I pushed her off me, and went into the bathroom to relieve myself, and when I came out she was pouting in the bed, grumbling about feeling rejected and that she needed to release. I opened her bedside table drawer and tossed her the vibrator that we used often when we fucked. She picked up the blue sex toy and threw it across the room.

She yelled. She didn't want that, but wanted to ride me. I got dressed, grabbed my bag and walked to the door, then told her I was too tired. As I walked to the front door of her apartment, she was screaming at me, but before I closed the door after stepping into the hallway, I heard the *humming* of the toy coming from the bedroom.

I strode to the side of the cage, grabbed my water bottle and drank half of it in one swallow. When I turned around, Rachel had her hands on hips and was glowering at me. Her brown eyes narrow, and her lips pinched together. She was frustrated that I stopped midway in the round, and I didn't give a shit. I needed a minute to calm down.

"C'mon, kid," Rachel taunted me.

Instead of listening to her, I raised the water bottle to my mouth and finished it. I tossed the empty bottle outside the cage and just stared at her. Seeing the fiery look she's giving me caused my shaft to throb. *Definitely not the time or place.* I willed it to grow flaccid, and bent over at the waist, placing my hands on my knees, inhaling and releasing my breath slowly. Once I had it under control, I stood and went back to the middle of the cage.

"Okay, c'mon," I held up my hands and began moving to the right. "Let's go."

We sparred for another thirty minutes before Rachel called the session over. I grabbed a towel, dried off my face and climbed under the rope to head over and grab more water. I'm amazed at how much water I drink nowadays. I had never been a water drinker before, but I felt as if I was dehydrated every minute of the day. These workouts and training sessions weren't only showing me I could be a fighter, but they were also allowing me to get into the best physical shape I'd ever been in.

My lanky body had muscle now. Gone was the flabby stomach fat, replaced with hard, toned muscle. My biceps had developed, and I could bench press more than I ever thought I'd be able to in my life.

My legs, which had been scrawny, were now muscle and more

flexible than I could recall. "Not bad for a runt," Rachel snorted as

she strolled past me.

I stepped in front of her, blocking her way, and my nose was within

inches of hers. "What the fuck is the matter with you?"

I could feel her breath on my face, and I knew she could feel mine, as

I was still heaving from the workout.

"Problem?" She smirked. "If you can't handle it, I suggest you move
on."

I wanted to say something, but all I could think about was taking her

by the waist, and throwing her down to the floor and fucking her.

Stripping her out of her clothes, kissing and tasting her skin while

my hand roamed up and down her glistening skin.

She pushed past me, shoving her shoulder into mine. I let her go, but

knew I'd have the last word soon enough.

My eyes traveled down her ass and hips as she strode away. The way
her hips moved had me
Entranced, as she moved away from me. I tried to stop the thoughts of

holding those hips as she rode me hard, grinding on my hard cock. The image was more than I could handle and headed to the shower. I needed to cool down my desire for her before I grabbed hold of my shaft and blew.

***

I left the gym with the intention of heading to the Blue Thunder for a beer, but when I went to my car to open the door, my eyes drifted up to Rachel's apartment. There was a light on, and instead of getting into my car, I strode to the stairs leading up to her place. Before I could stop myself, I was knocking on her door.

I could hear music playing, and seconds later, the door opened. I gasped inwardly when Rachel stood in front of me wearing nothing more than a sports bra and skimpy cotton shorts. I needed to know if she was wearing anything under the shorts.

"What do you want?" She snapped, leaning the side of her face against the door. "We need to talk," was all I could come up with to say. I had no idea why I came up here and needed an excuse to get in the door.

"Okay, so talk," she replied.

"Can I come in?"

"If you have to," she stepped aside, and I walked past her. I inhaled and could smell something like flowers.

"Okay, what do we need to talk about?" She asked, leaving the door wide open. "Your attitude," I stated.

"What about it?"

"I'm getting tired of your bullying bullshit," I said.

"Me? I'm not a bully," she snorted.

"I'm training you. If you can't handle what I'm giving you, you'll never make it in the cage."

"What you're giving me?" I exclaimed. "Are you freaking serious?"

"What?" She placed her balled fists on her hips, narrowing her eyes at me. "Do you honestly think an opponent won't try to sucker punch, or do another illegal move in the cage? Cause if you do, you're in for a rude awakening."

"At least if you're going to fight dirty, you can give me a heads-up," I countered. "Ha!" She chuckled.

"Like that's going to happen in an actual fight."

"So, a sneak attack is the best?" I cocked my head.

"Sure is, buddy," she replied.

"Like the other day in the hallway of the gym?" I lowered my voice.

"What the hell does that have to do with anything?" She scrunched her nose.

"This," I said, grabbing her around the waist, pulling her body to mine, and lowered my face to her. My mouth covered hers, and this time she didn't give me any resistance.

She wrapped her arms around my neck, and her fingers dug into my hair. When her lips parted slightly, my tongue darted into her mouth, and our kiss deepened. My hands wrapped around her waist, hoisted her up, and she locked her legs around my waist. Using my foot, I slammed the door she'd left open, and I strode to the sofa. I laid her down and took off my jacket.

I laid on top of her, moving my legs between hers, and captured her mouth with mine. As our lips parted, she moaned. My hand found her breast, and I slipped my hand under her bra. Moving the stretchy fabric aside, exposing her bosom. I lowered my head and sucked on her erect nipple. She grabbed my hair, holding my head there, as her hips moved, grinding into me.

Her hands left my head and began grappling at my shirt and pulling it up. When she got my shirt up to my chest, I stopped nibbling on her nipples and helped her get it off. Then I stood, unzipped my jeans and let them fall to the floor. I laid back on top of her and she instantly fumbled with my briefs to get them off.

We finished undressing in between kissing and touching each other, and when I slid between her legs, my shaft was throbbing. She took it in her hand and guided me into her. As soon as I entered her, she gasped and her hands grabbed my shoulders.

She ground her hips harder and spread her legs wider to allow me more access. With each thrust, she moaned and her breathing quickened. I placed a hand on her cheek and gazed into her eyes. When our eyes locked, I continued pounding into her harder.

"Oh yes," she gasped, licking her lower lip.

My breathing was coming harder, and I knew my release was

coming soon. I'd been imagining this moment for weeks, and how I'd go slow and savor every second of making love to her, but now that I was here, I wanted to go fast and feel the passion.

"Faster," she moaned.

Not needing any other prodding, my hips moved faster, and I tried to thrust deeper. Her hips moved, meeting every plunge I made. She wrapped her legs around my waist and we moved as one. "Oh, yes!" she yelled. "Yes!"

"Fuck!" I exclaimed as I came.

We slowed down, and once our bodies stopped, I collapsed onto her. Our bodies clung together from our perspiration, and I couldn't move because my legs were shaking. As our breathing returned to normal, I slid off her and grabbed my jeans.

Sliding one leg, then the other into my pants, Rachel sat on the edge of the sofa. She readjusted her bra and slipped her shorts back on. She stood, walked to the door, opened it, and glanced at me.

"Leave," she demanded. "This can never happen again."

"What?" I pulled my tee-shirt on and grabbed my jacket off the floor.

"You heard me," she answered. "Leave now."

"Are you serious?" I stood, walking towards her.

"Yes, on both accounts," she said. "Leave, and this will never happen again."
"What the fuck, Rachel!" I couldn't believe what I was hearing.

"We can't do this again," she said. "It was fun, and I feel better getting that out of my system, but it'll never happen again."

"Why not?"

"You know Johnny's rule," she replied, staring me down.

"He'll never know," I said.

"The hell he wouldn't," she snapped. "He'd know."

"Shit, Rachel," I was pissed.

I'd just had the best night of my life with a girl, and she was kicking me to the curb over some stupid rule that my uncle had put into place. The passion I had come over me just minutes ago was real, and Rachel wanted nothing to do with me again in this regard.

"Go!" she held the door open wider.

"Fine," I stomped past her. "But it *will* happen again."

She slammed the door and went down the stairs. I strode to my car in a huff, and just as I was about to open the door. When someone

came out of the shadows of the gym.

"Shit, dude," I gasped. "You scared the fuck out of me."

"Whatcha doing at Rachel's?" Liam grumbled.

"I had a score to settle with," I replied, and opened the

car door. "What's it to you?" "Don't get mixed up

with her," Liam warned. "She'll screw you over."

"I'm not getting involved with her," I replied.

"Better not," he said. "What beef did you have with her?"

"Not that it concerns you, but I needed to tell the bitch off," I said.

"Good," Liam nodded.

"Anything else?" I asked, putting one foot in the car.

"Naw," he replied. "See ya."
I watched him stroll back into the darkness and wondered how much

he knew about my visit to Rachel's place, and if he saw what

happened. I couldn't let the guy get to me. Whatever happened

between him and Rachel wasn't my business, and I wouldn't let it

deter me from getting with her. But if he knew what had just

happened up there, I'd need to curtail him from doing anything stupid.

Chapter 13

Rachel

I leaned against the door after Jack left, and I sighed. *What the hell just happened?* Not that I'm upset about sleeping with him. Not at all. I've been thinking about it way *too much* over the last few weeks. Every time I'd see Jack at the gym, or if we were working out and sparring, it didn't matter. My mind always went to how he'd be in bed.

"Been too long since you did the deed," I murmured.

But damn! Even though it was quick, it was fabulous! Incredible! It actually took my breath away.

Seeing Jack's muscles develop over the time we've been working together had been too much for me. The day he arrived at the gym and Johnny had put me on him as his trainer, I wasn't thrilled. But even when he was lanky, and had little to no muscle tone, I found myself attracted to him. I never figured out why. The only thing I could think of was because he was young, trim and had a quality about him that wasn't the norm that I'd consider being attracted to. He had a wholesome quality to him, and I preferred the *bad boy* attitude.

I reached over, locked the door and headed for the kitchen to grab a bottle of water. I felt dehydrated and grabbed a bottle of water off the counter. I still had a case of water that needed to be put in the refrigerator and mindlessly started doing that. Before too long, I was cleaning the kitchen, a chore I despised. Ever since I had that cleaning job years ago, I put off cleaning anything.

Being in such a small apartment, clutter seemed to accumulate quicker, so I spent another hour picking things up and decided tomorrow, after my time at the animal shelter, that I'd have to stop at the laundromat. I had more dirty clothes than clean ones.

As I shoved all the dirty clothes I'd scooped up into a hamper, I went into the tiny bathroom to shower. I needed to change and felt the need for a long, hot shower. While the hot water warmed up, my mind drifted to Jack and how full of passion he was. I wished we'd lasted longer, but I just needed a release, and he definitely helped in that area.

My only regret is how Johnny would react if, or when, he ever found out about it. The entire scene with Liam was still forefront in Johnny's mind. He never mentioned it, but I could see the skepticism on Johnny's face whenever Liam was around me. It was as if Johnny was waiting for an eruption between us.

For me, I avoided Liam, but no matter how much I ignored the man, he always seemed to be nearby, watching me with a sneer. I swore Liam did that because he knew how much it bothered me, as if he was waiting for me to react. But I wouldn't give him the pleasure of knowing how much it irritated me.

The only fighting I was going to be involved with happened in the cage. No more gym romances or love affairs to cloud my future. I'd learned a lesson, and now knew that having a relationship only clouded my judgment, and caused me to stay unfocused.

If I wanted to further my career and win another championship, I needed to remain fixated on it. No way was I going to allow a kid like Jack to ruin that for me.

"But damn," I murmured, as I stepped under the hot water. "He could be my undoing if I let it."

As I lathered up the soap and the water sluiced over my body, I imagined it was Jack's hands gliding over my body. I'd had this fantasy about Jack being in the shower with me too many times over the last few weeks, and it never got old. With every daydream, it was Jack touching me in another way. His hands moving over my wet skin, his fingers slipping between my legs, giving me pleasure. Staying in the shower longer than I had planned, I turned the water off and grabbed a clean towel to dry off. I got dressed and strode into my bedroom. I fell onto the bed and suddenly felt mentally and physically exhausted.

"Tomorrow's another day," I yawned, pulled a pillow under my head, and drifted off to sleep.

***

"C'mon!" I yelled at Jack. "Give me all you got!"

Shaking my head, I saw a fire develop in Jack's brown eyes. He was glaring at me after the last hit I threw at the side of his head. It pissed him off, and I was glad. It might not be fair, but I was taking out my aggression on him from our encounter a few nights ago. My adrenaline was still amped up, and I hadn't had a good workout since then.

"Bitch!" He glowered and raised his hands. "You want me to give it to you? Do ya!"

I wasn't sure if he was referring to our workout, or fucking again, but I didn't consider asking. Johnny was standing at the ropes watching us, and there's no way in hell I'd ever bring up the topic.

"Yeah, I do," I smirked. "I don't think you have it in you."

"I got it." Jack's eyes narrowed. "But I doubt you can handle it!"

"Go at her, Jack!" Johnny hollered. "Give her all you got!"

Jack laughed and came at me.

He jabbed from the right, then the left, and soon we were cradling each other, our heads touching and sweaty cheeks practically glued together.

"You want it?" Jack whispered. "You want it, don't you?"

Instead of replying, I pushed him off me and started bouncing from one leg to the other. I wiped my forehead with the back of my hand and glared at him.

"You don't have it," I seethed.

I couldn't believe he'd said that to me, right here, in front of Johnny. *What the fuck? Was he stupid?*

"Wanna bet!" He yelled. "I got it!"

"Then come at me!" I dared.

We spared for another ten minutes when the gym door opened, and I caught a glimpse of Jenna strolling in. She stopped to chat with two other male fighters before coming to the cage where Jack and I were. I could see her flirting with one of the guys, and snorted. Jenna was a piece of work, and I wondered if Jack knew of her promiscuous ways.

Just as the thought entered my head, Jack's hit caught me off guard, and my head flew back, causing me to lose my balance. I stumbled to the rope to help keep myself up.

"Yeah, I have it," Jack announced as Johnny clapped his hands.

"That's it, Jack," Johnny smiled. "Catch her off guard."

"He didn't catch me off guard," I spit out my mouthpiece. "I needed to see what kinda force he had."

"Yeah, right," Jack snickered, and strode to the rope, grabbed a towel and dried off his neck.

Just then Jenna came up to the cage, stood and stared at Jack. I glanced at Jack, who hadn't even noticed Jenna's presence. But

Johnny sure had. He lowered his shaking head and seemed pissed about the young girl being here.

"Okay, wrap it up," Johnny yelled. "Jack?" He cocked his head towards the side of the cage.

Jack tossed his towel down and walked to where Johnny stood.

I walked to the corner of the cage, grabbed a water bottle and popped it open. As I guzzled the water down, I kept one ear trained on Johnny and Jack's conversation.

"You need to get a handle on her," Johnny said. I assumed he was referring to me.

"Man," Jack bowed his head as he undid his gloves. "I can't control when she comes here."

Ah, not me, but Jenna. Interesting.

"You need to tell her to steer clear," Johnny said. "You gotta fight coming up soon, and I don't need pussy coming between you and that win."

"It's not," Jack replied. "I won't let it."

"Talk to her," Johnny pointed his finger at Jack. "You lose the fight because of her?" Johnny shook his head. "You're outta here."

"I'm not planning on losing," Jack stated.

"You better not," Johnny replied. "Either way, she needs to go. I already told you about this shit, and how I won't tolerate it."

"Yeah, you said no sex between people in the gym," Jack snorted.

"But Jenna's not with the gym."

"Yeah, but she comes by too often, and some of the guys don't need her in here. She's too much of a distraction."

I glanced at Jenna and saw what Johnny meant. She had that perfect pout on her face that I'm sure most men fell for. Her blonde hair, that I assumed came from a bottle every few weeks, to her upturned nose. Jenna was the type of girl to make men do things they probably wouldn't do. And that's not something anyone would ever mistake me for, someone like Jenna.

I may not turn the heads of too many guys, but I didn't really rely on my looks to get a man. If a guy didn't like, or want, me for who I was, screw him, was my motto.

"Okay, okay," Jack said. "I'll talk to her."

Then Johnny walked to his office, closing the door.

I finished the bottle of water, avoiding eye contact with Jack, as I didn't want him to know I'd heard what Johnny said. I tossed the empty bottle in the garbage can beside the cage and climbed through the ropes.

I sat on the bench, removing my headgear, gloves and tape, watching Jack stroll towards Jenna. They talked for a few minutes, and when Jenna's lips turned to a frown, I knew he'd told her she had to steer clear of the gym.

Thank God. I shook my head. I didn't care about seeing the girl either, so I'm thankful to Johnny for putting his foot down.

I finished unwrapping the tape off my wrists, and tossed it in the garbage can, and wished I had another bottle of water in my bag. Jack draped his arm over Jenna's shoulder and escorted her out of the gym.

Good riddance.

I picked up my bag and headed for a shower. This workout had been intense, and I chalked it up to my libido being high ever since screwing Jack. It's amazing how much I forgot how much I liked sex when I wasn't having it. But now that I've had a taste of it, and Jack, I hated myself for wanting more.

***

"Now what?" I grumbled, setting my microwave meal on the table beside the sofa. I'd just got it heated up and was settling in to eat the bland meal when someone knocked on the door. I glanced at the clock hanging on the kitchen wall and saw it was half past ten. I was tired from the day's workouts, but I also hadn't eaten anything all day, so eating this meal took precedence over sleep.

I stood, walked to the door, whipped it open, and saw Jack leaning against the door frame.

"What the hell do you want?" I scowled more at it being him, then at the interruption.

"Came by to tell you that I couldn't sleep," He mumbled.

"And that's my problem, how?" I planted my balled fists onto my hips.

"I was going to go for a walk to clear my head," he grinned. "But saw your light on."

"And?" I sighed.

"I figured I'd see what you were up to," he shrugged.

"Where's Jenna?"

"No clue," he snorted.

"So instead of going to be with her, you thought you'd bother me?"

"Pretty much," his grin came back.

"Well, joke's on you then," I cocked my head. "I was just about to head off to bed."

He glanced over my shoulder. "Looks like you're about to eat."

"I'm tired, Jack," I sighed. "Is that all?" I began to close the door, but he stepped inside, blocking the door.

"Heading off to bed sounds good," he smiled.

"Alone," I spat.

"Too bad," he murmured. "I have a lot of pent up energy."

"Again, not my problem," I glared at him. "Go find Jenna."

"I don't want her," he murmured. "I want you."

"Maybe I don't want you," I lied.

"I think you do." he stepped closer, then closed the door.

"Jack, I told you the other night, it was a onetime thing," I muttered.

"It wasn't," he lowered his head, wrapped an arm around my waist, pulling my body to him. His mouth covered mine, and I couldn't help but respond.

"Bedroom," I murmured in between our kisses.

He grabbed under my ass, hoisted me up, and carried me to my bedroom. He set me on the bed, stripped out of his clothes, as I removed my shorts and tank top. He crawled onto the bed, lowered me back, and soon his lips found mine again. My arms went around his neck, and I gave into the passion still running hot within me. Jack ran one of his hands down the length of my body, and as his hand slid over my hip, I groaned. He slid his hand as far down as he could on my outer thigh, and I had no control over the movement of my hips.

He pulled his lips off mine, gazed into my eyes, and I lost all common sense about this never happening again. The only thoughts I had were to make love to Jack, and never want it to end.

He lowered his body, and his lips found my nipples, and he began sucking on them. Once erect, his teeth gently nibbled them. This caused my body to shower, and I arched my back. My hands dug into his hair, and I lulled back.

"Mmm," I moaned, enjoying his teasing. As I shifted my body, Jack slid his hand between my legs, and quickly found my pleasure area.

"Oh, yes."

He moved his mouth to my other breast and continued his torture. My hips began moving, pushing against him, demanding more.

His mouth released my nipple, and he began moving down my abdomen, kissing every inch that he could. When he got to my mound, I kept my hands on the top of his head, guiding him to where we both wanted him to go.

"Oh, God," I murmured, thrashing my head.

Jack continued taunting and teasing me before moving on to my wetness. His tongue slid across me, then began flicking through my folds.

"Yes!" I exclaimed. "I need you inside me."

Without responding, Jack moved his body up to mine and positioned himself between my thighs. I spread my legs further, allowing him more room. Pressing up on his arms, I felt his throbbing shaft against my inner thigh.

He grabbed his member and found me. He thrust deep, and I felt his hard shaft within me. My body shuddered and accepted his length. As he began moving, my hips met with each plunge.

"Damn it," he swore, as he placed both hands beside my head, using his arms as leverage to continue pumping into me.

"Yes!" I panted, grabbing his ass with each hand and pulling him into me.

"You want it," he growled.

"Yes, give it to me," I exclaimed.

His thrust grew faster and deeper. With each push, he grunted, and his throbbing shaft pounded into me, and I could feel my orgasm growing closer.

"Yes, Jack!" I squeezed his ass cheeks and held on as my climax erupted.

"Fuck yeah," Jack roared as he released. His hips slowed down, and I felt his body tremble. When he was done, he pushed off me and rolled to my side. His body collapsed to the bed, and I could hear him breathing hard.

My heart was beating fast, and I tried to regain my breathing. I glanced over to the bedside table and cussed when I didn't see a bottle of water there.

"Damn it," I sighed. "I need water."

"Me too," he said. He got out of bed, strode out of the room. When he returned, he had two bottles of water, and handed me one of them. We both opened the bottle and drank.

"Better than the last time," he said.

"Yeah," I panted. "Definitely."

"So much for it being a one-time thing," he chuckled.

"I'm serious, Jack," I replied. "We can't let this keep happening. You need to stop coming here."

"I can't," he said.

"You know, I heard you and Johnny talking earlier," I said.

"Yeah, and?"

"He told you about messing around," I replied, drinking more water.

"He won't know," Jack replied. "I'm not telling him."

"He'll know," I mumbled. "Then there'll be a problem."

"We'll deal with it when it happens," he replied.

"Be too late then," I sat up. "This ends now."

"So, you're going to miss out on the best lay you've ever had because of some stupid ass rule?"

"Yes," I hissed. "It's my career," I stated. "And I'm not going to lose it over you."

"Fine," Jack sat up, leaned over and grabbed his clothes. "You'll come begging me for more."

"Doubt it," I snapped.

"We'll see," he said, as he pulled up his jeans, then slipped on his shirt.

"Don't come here again, Jack," I replied. "I mean it."

"Whatever," he shrugged, slipped into his shoes, and left the bedroom.

I heard the door close in his wake and sat there with my knees bent and my elbows resting on them.

"Good job, Corvi," I scolded myself. "You're such an idiot."

Chapter 14

Jack

"Man, that was a good one." I climbed out of the cage and slapped my hand into Johnny's hand.

"Looking good," Johnny nodded. "You fight like that next week, and you're gonna fucking win."

"Hell yeah!" I yelled.

"Damn," Johnny shook his head. "Didn't think you had it in you."

"What the hell?" I laughed, drinking from my water bottle.

"Just being honest," Johnny shrugged. "Hey, Rachel, you did a fan-freakin-tastic job!"

I glanced at Rachel, who was watching from the other side of the cage. She had me spar with another fighter instead of her today, as she wanted to see how I did with someone I wasn't familiar with. She made a good choice in the guy I just pounded on the mat. While it wasn't Liam, for some reason, while I was in the cage, I kept picturing Liam, and it didn't take me long before I had the guy down.

Maybe that's what I needed to do next week when I entered the cage for my fight. *Just imagine it was Liam I was going against.*

"Damn straight," Rachel hollered. "You did good, Jack!" She nodded at me.

I sat on the bench, watched as Rachel chatted with her trainer, Josh. They were holding their hands up and acting as if they were making moves. *Probably working out some kinks in her own training sessions.*

"Mother offer," Johnny slapped my back. "You've proved yourself in the cage just now."

"Thanks, Johnny," I nodded. "Means a lot to me, but it'd mean more if you had faith in me from the start."

"Gotta prove yourself," he shook his head. "Some people are naturals, and some aren't. I didn't think you were a natural."

"Glad I could fucking prove you wrong," I laughed.

"Me too," Johnny said. "I've been pumping up your fight, and after that show, I have no doubts you'll be cleaning up the place."

"Can't wait," I nodded.

"So, you still pissed about having a female trainer?" Johnny roared.

"Fuck no!" I shook my head. "Best decision I ever made."

"You?" Johnny chuckled. "Of course, you'd take credit for it *now*."

"You know it," I stood, and walked over to the cage, placing my forearms on the ropes, and watching the fighters in it now. No sooner did I leave the cage, the next two guys stepped in for their sparring. Johnny joined me, and we stood in silence watching the guys fight and go over moves.

"She's the best at her craft," Johnny nodded towards Rachel.

"Yeah, she is," I replied. "Sorry I doubted you."

"You should be," he chuckled. "You two seem to be getting along better."

"Yeah, I guess we came to an agreement," I nodded. "Seems like we got over the bad part."

"Makes it easier, for sure," Johnny replied.

I glanced at Rachel, and she was still talking to Josh. They were pretty involved, and I felt jealousy come over me. They were standing close to one another, and when Josh placed his hands on her shoulders, I wanted to march over and take a swing at the guy.

But I knew that would not only cause Rachel to get furious, but it would raise questions from Johnny about why I was being so protective over her. That's the last thing I needed to have happened.

Rachel glanced in my direction and rolled her eyes. I suppose my disgruntled face gave her the idea that I didn't care for Josh being so physical with her. I shook my head and glimpsed at Johnny. Maybe if I talked to him about what's happening between me and Rachel, he'd understand. Perhaps he'd given me a *pass* since I'm his nephew.

"Sonofabitch," Johnny grumbled.

"What?" I asked.

"Fucking Liam," he nodded towards another cage.

I glanced in the direction and saw Liam scowling at Rachel. "What's up with that?"

"His freaking jealousy," Johnny shook his head. "Gotta keep my eye on him."

"Why's he such a dick to her?"

"He's too possessive for his own good," Johnny replied. "I don't think he ever got over her."

I nodded, and glimpsed at Rachel, who had no idea Liam was glaring at her. "She gets over him/"

"She was over him before it started," Johnny chuckled. "She's a helluva fighter, but she's not a wonderful lover."

"What's that mean?" I asked.

"Just like I said," Johnny moved his eyes back to Liam. "She's not a commitment kind woman."

"Afraid of commitment?"

"No, she eats commitment for breakfast," he replied. "She doesn't know how to be in a relationship as far as I can figure."

I nodded again, and stared at Rachel, who was packing up her bag, and would probably be heading off to the locker room soon.

"Hey, Johnny," Liam approached.

"Yeah, what's up?"

I sensed Johnny tensing up when Liam came up to us. His fingers tightened around the rope, and I saw his face grow stoic.

"Got a minute?" Liam asked.

"Yeah, whatcha need?"

"In your office?" Liam bore his eyes into me.

"Yeah, only got a few minutes, so make it quick," Johnny replied, pushed off the rope and headed for his office.

As Liam passed me, his eyes remained locked with mine, as if challenging me. I didn't glance away, as I wanted him to know I wasn't intimidated by him at any level.

The guy wasn't right in the head. It was as if he were a loose cannon ready to blow. When I first met him, he seemed like a nice enough guy, but over the last couple of months, I've seen some weird behavior from him that bothered me.

When he learned Rachel was my trainer, he warned me not to get involved with her. At the time, I assumed she was a bad person, but as time went on, I didn't perceive her as what he told me. Granted, they had dated, and no relationship ends without bitter feelings and negative words, but Liam took things to the extreme.

Like the first time me and Rachel screwed, and Liam was outside the gym just hanging around. That bothered me for days. When I left her apartment the other night, I made sure Liam wasn't lurking in the shadows before I went down the stairs. I kept my head on a swivel, watching for him until I was inside the gym, and settled into my room.

When Liam reached Johnny's office, he entered and closed the door.

It wasn't as if anyone could hear their conversation, because the noise in the gym superseded over everything. Johnny had the blinds still open, and I could see Liam start talking.

After a few minutes, Johnny held up his hand to stop Liam from talking and shook his head. Liam threw his hands in the air, and I could tell he was getting pissed. He began pacing the office, waving his hands, and appeared to be yelling. Johnny's mouth was moving, too.

I trained my ears on the scene unfolding in the office, but I couldn't pick up anything being said. Between the yelling, music and people fighting in the gym, the office argument was lost in the noise.

"What's that jackass doing now?" Josh, Rachel's trainer, strolled up beside me.

"Not a clue," I mumbled, glimpsing at the guy. The same guy I was jealous of ten minutes ago.

"Always up to no good." Josh crossed his arms over his broad chest.

"Is he?"

"Fuck yeah." Josh shook his head. "He's the typical *keep your enemies closer* kinda, dude."

"Back stabber?"

"Naw, nothing like that," Josh replied. "But he'll fuck you over the first chance he gets."

I nodded.

"I still don't know why Johnny didn't keep him outta here after the whole Rachel thing," Josh shrugged. "But it's not my business. But that guy's bad news."

"So I've been hearing," I nodded.

"Well, see ya later." Josh patted my back and headed off to one of his fighters.

I watched Josh walk away, and realized my jealousy of him wasn't a problem. But I could envision Liam being a huge complication, especially if he saw me leaving Rachel's place.

"Definitely need to keep him close at hand," I took Josh's warning to heart.

I needed to decide if I was going to talk to Johnny about me and Rachel, but before that, I needed to know how much Liam knew.

<u>Chapter 15</u>

Rachel

I watched Liam follow Johnny into the office, and I knew something

was up, and it wasn't something good. Johnny disappeared into his

office, and Liam stopped in the doorway, glanced at me, and winked. I

felt nauseated. My stomach felt sour, and bile rose up in my throat,

burning. I rubbed my hand across my neck and swallowed hard.

I scanned the gym for Jack, but saw him talking to Josh. They were in

what appeared to be a deep conversation, and as frantic as I felt, I

didn't want to disrupt them. I'd come out of the hallway that led to the

locker rooms and shower areas when I saw Liam and Johnny walking

across the gym.

Normally this wouldn't have fazed me, but considering what's been

going on between me and Jack the last week, the hairs on the back of

my neck stood up.

I waited a few minutes, and when Josh walked away from Jack, I

made a beeline for him.

"What's up with that?" I tossed my head to the side, indicating Johnny's office.

"No frickin' clue," he replied, and began unwrapping his hands. "But I don't trust the jerk."

"You're preaching to the choir," I replied, my eyes trained on Johnny's office.

I could see them still talking, and Liam was animated, and pacing the floor. Johnny was leaning against his desk, arms crossed over his chest, and appearing a little irritated with Liam. I took Johnny's frustration with Liam as a good sign. Liam was hopefully blabbering, and being the typical jerk-off we all knew him to be, and Johnny was just pacifying him by listening.

"I was thinking about talking to Johnny too," Jack said as he sat on the bench.

"About what?" My head snapped to stare at him.

"About us. This," he waved his hand between them.

"Oh, fuck no," I growled. "Don't even go there. There is *no* us."

"Think what you want, Rachel," he replied. "But there is something here."

"Even if there was," I hissed. "It's not going anywhere."

"You're full of shit," he chuckled. "It's going somewhere."

"Jack," I growled. "You go to Johnny about this, and my career with the gym is over. You hear me? It's over."

"I doubt it," he replied. "You get all worked up over stupid crap. Johnny won't care."

"You weren't here when all that shit went down with Liam," I pointed a finger at him. "You think, just because you're his family, that you're immune. But you're not."

"No, I wasn't here when that shit happened," he said. "But I've heard about it."

"You hear the rumors." I stepped closer to him. "You weren't in the office when Johnny ripped my ass out. You didn't see how tense things were in the gym."

"You're blowing all this up," he replied, and stood.

We were eye to eye, and if I wasn't so pissed off, I'd get lost in his brown eyes. There was something about his gaze that caused my stomach to *flip-flop*, but I needed to set those feelings aside, and make him understand there was *no us*.

"If Johnny even suspects we're fucking around, he'll toss me outta here faster than the speed of light," I hissed. "But you don't get it. I didn't put all this time, and all these years, into my career for you to ruin it."

"I'm not ruining anything," he spat. "I just don't want to keep running around. I don't want to sneak around anymore."

"There will be no more sneaking around," I said. "There is no us."

"You know there is," he said. "You just haven't realized it yet."

"What the fuck, Jack," I sneered. "How old are you? We're not some junior or senior high school kids here. We're adults!"

My voice raised, and I scanned around the gym to see who was nearby, or listening to us. The noise of the fighters and trainers seemed to be drowning out our conversation, and I didn't see anyone glancing in our direction. This relieved me, and I sighed.

"You're just too uptight." Jack shook his head. "But I have the remedy for that."

"Shut the fuck up, Jack," I seethed. "Stop acting like a child."

He stepped closer to me, leaned down and whispered, "There is an us, and we *will* continue on."

"I liked you better when you were a simple kid," I scowled. "When you had no balls, and were afraid of your own shadow."

"Those days are long gone, baby," he tossed his head back, laughing. "What you get now is the true Jack Garrett. Take it or leave it."

"I'll leave it," I spun around, stomping to the locker room, but glimpsing into Johnny's office to see him and Liam still talking.

"Hey!" Jack hollered.

I stopped, turned my head to see what he wanted.

"I get it," he yelled. "For now."

I sighed and continued marching away. I needed to shower and think. I didn't trust Jack to hold true to his word, but I couldn't do anything to convince him not to talk to Johnny, short of breaking the law. But I wasn't about to let Jack wreck everything I've been working so hard to create over the last few years.

So much blood, sweat and tears went into being a champion fighter, and I could kick myself for allowing another relationship to take over my desire to add a second championship title to my name. I learned a lesson with Liam, or so I thought.

Chapter 16

Jack

"Damn it, Jack!" Johnny screamed. "Where the hell is your head?"

"Fuck!" I yelled, and spit out my mouthpiece into my gloved hand.

"Damn it, Rachel! What the hell are you doing?"

"Making sure you're ready for your first fight!" She shouted. "You don't need to go out into the cage in two days and get slammed in the first few minutes."

"I'm not planning to." I shoved the mouth guard back in. "Let's go again."

"This time, watch!" Johnny yelled. "Don't let her get the best of you!"

I glimpsed at Johnny, who was resting his forearms on the rope and had his chin resting on his entwined hands. He seemed to have aged a lot since my arrival a few months ago. His brown hair appeared to have more gray developing than I remembered.

"Come at me!" Rachel yelled.

I turned my attention to her, and she had her hands up, and was shifting her weight from one leg to the other. I wiped my brow with my gloved hand, raising both hands in preparation to wallop her ass. I wasn't going to let her show me up.

"Go, Jack!" Johnny hollered.

I skipped forward, and held my left hand up closer to my face, while my right hand was more level to my chest. I took a few more steps, and Rachel moved to her right, and we circled each other. Out of nowhere, Rachel jabbed her right hand, and I was ready this time. Using my left hand, I blocked her, then my right hand sprung out, connecting with her left ear.

"Good," Johnny clapped. "Keep it up!"

We did this *dance* for another minute, when Rachel ducked down and came at me. I lowered both my hands and pushed her way, raising my right leg, and knocking her backwards when my foot caught her in the gut.

"Yeah!" Johnny clapped.

Rachel stood, rubbed her stomach, and I thought she was smirking.

But I didn't give her a reprieve, as I pounced and thrust my left hand at her head. She was too slow to block the impending punch, and she fell back onto the rope. She shook her head and held up a hand.

"Hang on," she shouted.

"That's it, Jackie boy!" Johnny yelled. "Yeah!"

"Take five," Rachel hollered.

"No," I replied. "Keep going."

"Fine," she hissed, and came at me..

We sparred for another half hour, and only stopped when Johnny clapped his hands and called it.

"Great session," Johnny said, slapping my back when I sat on the stool in the corner.

Grabbing a water bottle, I drank half its contents and nodded.

"Yeah, good one," Rachel walked up.

"I'm ready to go again," I glanced at her. "Are you?"

I knew she got the double meaning to my statement, and I snickered.

She glared at me and placed her hands on her hips.

"Ha," she tossed her head back. "You barely got through that one."

"Hey," I scowled. "I had some good punches, and you even asked for a break."

"True," she nodded. "But you don't have the stamina."

Damn! She was dishing it out just as well. I was impressed. Johnny, who was none the wiser, laughed.

"You two sound like an old married couple," he roared, slapping my back again. "Now I see why you clobbered each other out there."

"Yeah," I mumbled. "If I was married to her, I'd be slamming her."

"You're an asshole." Rachel shook her head.

"So you keep saying," I chuckled, and Rachel shot me daggers from her eyes.

"I don't care why you two hate each other so much," Johnny interrupted. "But keep it up."

Johnny strode away, and headed to the cage next to the one we were in, and I finished drinking my water. Rachel walked away, going to the opposite corner of the cage, where her bag was on the edge of the platform. She bent over, and her skin-tight shorts molded to her ass, and my cock twinged, causing me to growl.

"Dammit," I muttered, and put my head back, averting my eyes from the view.

"Not bad," Liam said from behind me.

I rolled my eyes, as I didn't want to deal with him right now. I didn't trust the guy, and having him around bothered me.

"What do you want?"

"Nothing." he rested his arms on the rope. "Just checking out your progress."

I nodded, as I hoped he'd just leave.

"Surprised you did so well today, considering all the late nights you've been keeping."

I knew where he was going with this conversation, and I wanted nothing to do with it. I grabbed my bag, stood and climbed out of the ropes.

"Where are you going?" He asked.

"To shower," I mumbled.

"Drinks later?"

"No, thanks," I grumbled.

"Hey, why not?"

"I need to get some rest," I said. "First fight in two days."

"Oh, come on," Liam pushed. "One drink."

"Not tonight," I began walking away.

"Why not? You got a date or something?"

I stopped walking, turned to come face to face with him. "What I do in my personal life is none of your fucking business."

"Hey, hey," he held up his hands. "No drinks. Damn, you're high strung."

"I've got a lot on my mind."

"I bet," he sneered, and when I glanced at him, he was staring at Rachel.

I glimpsed in her direction and saw she was climbing out of the cage, then headed towards the door leading to the showers.

"Go away, Liam," I hissed. "I don't need any distractions from you or anyone else right now."

"Distractions?" He darted his eyes back to me. "You need to get laid. That'll get you some relief from the stress. I always give a good pounding before I fight."

"Yeah, whatever," I shook my head.

"Solid advice, man," he laughed, then walked away. "You should take it!" He continued laughing as he headed for the locker room. He disappeared behind the door seconds after Rachel went through the same door.

I headed for my room instead of the shower. I didn't want to see Liam right now. I'd shower later, then I'd head out for dinner. After that session and the workout earlier, I was starving. But all that would have to wait.

***

I pulled my car into the gym's parking lot after I'd gone to the little store around the corner. I had planned on getting a real meal, but knew I shouldn't. I needed to stick to my strict diet so I wouldn't have to steam weight off before weigh-in tomorrow. It's bad enough tomorrow would be a cleansing day, and no food allowed, but I didn't want to spend ten hours in the sauna to lose a few pounds. I was only two-pounds over my weight limit and knew the fasting from now until weigh-in would be enough to get me to the weight I needed to be. I haven't had the sauna experience yet, but I'd seen the fighters who had, and I wanted nothing to do with it. No way, that wasn't for me. I wasn't going to suffer and put my body through that crap.

I climbed out of the car, grabbed the bag of nuts, sweet potatoes for myself after the fight meal, and other healthy low-calorie foods and began walking to the gym's back door. Midway to the door, I stopped.

I turned my direction and headed up to Rachel's apartment.

Her light was on, and I knew she'd be there. She rarely went out, as

I'd only seen her a few times the Blue Thunder.

"Perhaps I can liven up her night," I smiled, as I climbed the steps.

I knocked on the door, and she opened almost immediately.

"Jesus, Jack, now what do you want?" She was wearing what

appeared to be a man's oversized tee-shirt, and I imagined her naked

beneath it. Just the thought of that sent my desire into a tizzy.

"Came to show you the stamina I still have."

"Go away," she started to close the door, but I stepped inside.

"No," I said, dropping the plastic grocery bag on the floor. "Not until I

release some pent-up energy."

"I told you no more." she crossed her arms over her chest,

emphasizing her full breasts.

"Just one more time," I replied. "Come on, I need to release."

"Go find Jenna," she snarled.

"I don't want her, and I'm already here."

"Dammit, Jack," she sighed. "If Johnny hears about this, and with Liam scoping things out a little too close, this is a huge mistake."

I stepped closer, placing my hands on her hips, and didn't feel a panty line, causing my shaft to throb and grow stiff.

"But that's not a no," I murmured. "Just a *we have to be careful*."

"This needs to be the last time," she whispered.

She gazed into my eyes and shut the door. She wrapped her arms around my neck, and I lowered my hands, grabbing her ass, and hoisted her up. She encircled my waist with her legs, and I stumbled, carrying her to the bedroom.

This wasn't going to be the last time, as she said. This was only the beginning.

<u>Chapter 17</u>

Rachel

Today started out great, as I woke up feeling refreshed and completely void of stress. I had to give most of this relief to Jack for exhausting me last night, but the other part of it was that I was no longer full time in my training of him. He had his first fight tomorrow, and aside from last-minute workouts or advice, my time with Jack had come to an end.

It's a bittersweet moment actually, but knowing I could now focus on my own training, and get back into the cage for my own fight coming up in two months, made me feel as if I was walking lighter.

That positive mood evaporated quickly when I strolled into the gym, only to be greeted by Johnny glaring at me and nodding his head towards his office.

In comparison to being called to the principal's office in high school, this was not good. My stomach *flipped*, and I felt a strange nausea rise in my stomach, causing a sour taste in my mouth.

I set my bag on a bench near a cage and followed Johnny into his office. Once I stepped inside, he asked me to close the door. I did, then I turned to face whatever bitching out I was about to receive.

"You know how I feel about this shit, Rachel," he said as he sat in the chair behind his desk. His elbows rested on the desk, and his hands steepled in front of him.

"About what, exactly?"

"About fucking around here."

"What did Liam say?" I suspected that the bastard had said something the other day, but I didn't think he'd actually do it. Being so underhanded wasn't going to win Liam any brownie points with me, and I wouldn't give in to blackmail for us to get back together. The guy was a nutjob, and had to know by now we were never going to be a couple again.

"You're assuming it was Liam," Johnny shook his head.

In my head, I started thinking who else would've known about me and Jack, and that was it. Those are the only two people that I knew of who had insider information that we were carrying on.

Me and Jack.

"Mother fucker," I seethed. "Who told you?"

"Doesn't matter," Johnny stated. "You know the rules. Hell, you're the reason for the rule."

"Johnny, come on," I approached his desk. "I've been training Jack, as per your request, and now I'm getting ready for my own training and fight."

"Stop," he held up his hand.

"Johnny..."

"No," he shook his head. "Pack your locker up."

"What the fuck, Johnny?" my voice quivered as I felt tears forming. "You can't be serious!"

"Now, Rachel," he replied. "I'm not going to listen to any story, excuse or lie." He stood and walked towards the office door, but as he passed me, he said, "You have ten minutes."

"My place?" I growled.

"By tonight," then he left the office.

I balled my hands into fists, and wanted to start screaming and punching anything, or someone, but instead I leveled my breathing, loosened my hands and walked out of the office. I wouldn't give anyone the opportunity to see my rage.

As I passed the bench, I grabbed my bag and headed for the locker room. I didn't have too much in my locker, but I'd be out of here in less than five minutes. As I marched across the gym, my eyes came in direct line with Liam, who was smirking across the room.

I glared at him and knew at that instant he had been the one who told Johnny about me and Jack.

I slammed through the swinging door leading to the locker room, and only when I got to where my locker was located at the back of the room did I let a few tears fall. I held back from punching a fist into the metal locker, as I knew that would only hurt me more. A hand injury could ruin my career, and I wasn't about to let Liam take that from me as well.

After cleaning out my locker, I sighed and fought back the tears as I reached for the door leading out into the gym. I needed to just walk straight out, with my head held high and not make eye contact with anyone.

So, that's what I did.

Once outside, I jogged to the stairs and climbed up to my apartment. As I packed p my belongings, I called a female fighter I knew from another gym that I was friends with. I told her I needed a place to crash for a few days, and without asking any questions, she said to come on over.

I left the key to the place on the table, grabbed my bags and closed the door. As I made my way across the parking lot, I saw Jack's car was absent from his usual spot, and figured I'd call him after I got to my friend's place. Not that there was anything he could do for me, but I needed to forewarn him about what went down.

Two hours later, I dialed Jack's number but got his voicemail. I'm assuming he's in the weigh-in process for his fight tomorrow, so I left him a voicemail.

I had no idea if he'd get the message before going back to the Rogue Warriors, but I did all I could do. I spent the rest of the evening drowning my sorrows in a few drinks, and letting my mind wander. Every time Jack and I hooked up, I felt myself growing more and more attracted to him. Despite our age difference, he made me feel years younger than I really was. Jack could make me laugh at the most inopportune times, and I'd noticed my happier outlook on life since he'd arrived.

Granted, we could go round and round in heated arguments and squabbles, but isn't that how things go for couples?

Couples? Where the hell did that come from? We weren't a couple!

I finally had to admit to myself that I had fallen in love with Jack. As much as I fought the feelings, or the urge, it was undeniable. I guess now that I was no longer a member of Rogue Warriors, we could carry on as much as we wanted. But I had no idea how Jack truly felt.

"No more drinking for you," I murmured, shaking my head, and setting the bottle of vodka aside.

Chapter 18

Jack

"Hey, Johnny!" I hollered over the roar of the crowd. "Where's Rachel?"

Johnny held up a finger, telling me he'd be over in a minute, and I continued to get my fingers and hands wrapped. The cage trainer had come to me about ten minutes ago, and started wrapping me, and when I asked the guy where Rachel was, all he did was shrug.

I kept my head on a pivot for the last half hour, scanning the seats in the arena for Rachel. I had no idea where she was, why she wasn't wrapping my hands or here to give me a pep talk, and I was getting pissed that she blew me off, today of all days.

Johnny came over, tapped the trainer on the shoulder, and cocked his head so he'd leave.

"Where the fuck is Rachel?" I hissed.

"She's not coming, I suppose."

"What do you mean, you suppose she's not coming? What the hell happened?"

"You know why," Johnny glared at me. "I had to let her go."

"Let her go!" I yelled. "Why'd you do that?"

"She knew the rules, and the only reason I didn't boot your ass to the curb is because you're family," Johnny sneered.

"Mother fucker!" I screamed as Johnny walked away and slipped out of the cage.

The trainer came back over, finished his job, then I turned to see who my coach was, and saw Josh standing there. I shook my head, and as the referee came into the cage, I took one final glance around the arena, but still didn't see Rachel.

My fury was forefront, and I knew I was going to pummel the guy I was fighting. All my rage was bursting at the seams, and I was on the verge of exploding. I honestly felt sorry for my opponent.

***

When Josh hugged me in the cage after my win, my heart was pounding out of my chest. I took a minute to search for Rachel again, and at the last second, I saw her on the runway, above the first section of seats. She was standing in the doorway, and the only reason I was able to see her was because of the lights illuminating her body from the concourse.

I called out, yelling the loudest I could to get her attention, but she'd already turned and left.

People were coming up to me left and right. I heard a few of the guys introduce themselves from being associated with other gyms, but I barely listened, as my mind was on getting to Rachel.

"Dammit!" I screamed as Johnny came up and hugged me.

"You did good, kid," He smacked the side of my headgear. "You won!"

"Yeah," I spit out my mouthpiece and tried to move away, and go in the direction I'd seen Rachel, but too many people stood in the way, and Johnny grabbed my arm, pulling me back.

"Hey, hey," Johnny hollered. "Com'ere."

"I need to go." I pulled my arm free.

"Where to?"

"To find Rachel." I shoved myself against him, our noses touching.

"She was here."

"Get outta my face, you punk," he growled.

"Kiss my ass," I said, removing my headgear. "It's because of you she wasn't able to be out there with me!"

"Dammit, Jack," he shook his head.

"No!" I yelled. "I'm not talking right now."

"What the hell, Jack."

"Listen here," I began ranting. "I'm more than pissed off at you for what you did to Rachel, and then *not* telling me until the fight. That's a bullshit move!"

"What? And have me tell you when then?" Johnny grabbed my shirt.

I pulled from his grasp and held my hand up to punch him. "Don't *ever* grab me like that again!"

"Calm down." Johnny held up his hands.

We spent the next ten minutes talking, or more like arguing, and when I threatened to leave the gym, he started to call my bluff, when a man approached us, and introduced himself as Lyle Victors. I had no clue who the guy was, and was about to tell him to get the hell away from me, and his next words shocked the hell out of me.

<u>Epilogue</u>

After the fight I went to find Rachel, and luckily the fighting

community was pretty tight, and I was knocking on the door of

another female fighter hours after my win. Rachel opened the door,

and as soon as she saw me, she leaped out the door and landed in my

arms. Her lips captured mine, and she waited for me to lift her up.

Once I did, her legs were wrapped around my waist.

"You freaking won!" she exclaimed when our lips parted.

"Damn straight I did!" I roared and set her down.

"I'm so happy for you," she kissed me again.

"It was a team effort," I nodded.

"I was there," she bit her lip.

"I looked for you."

"You never would've seen me," she sighed. "I stayed back so I

wouldn't have to deal with Johnny, Liam... or anyone else."

"I get it." I stepped inside the little apartment. While he had seen her

after the win, and he tried to get through the crowds to get to her, he

couldn't break free from the congratulations and people fawning over him. But saw no reason to mention it. "I got some more news."

"What's that?" she asked, closing the door.

"I was thinking about leaving the Rogue Warriors."

"You can't do that," she yelled. "Just because I'm gone doesn't mean you need to leave."

"Yeah, it does," I shrugged.

"Dammit, Jack," she scowled. "Why would you go and do something so stupid?"

"I don't know."

"You go back there," she pointed out the door, "And tell Johnny you made a mistake. This is the beginning of your career, and I won't let you throw it all away because of me!"

"Me and Johnny talked," I said. "We came to an agreement."

"An agreement?" she narrowed her eyes.

"Well, more of an ultimatum."

"What the hell are you talking about?"

"I told him if he didn't let you come back to the gym, then I was outta there."

"Good God, Jack," she began pacing, and had her hands over her face.

"Why the hell would you do that?"

"Cause I won't train where you're not," I shrugged.

She stopped pacing, stared at me, and shook her head. "You're an idiot."

"I may be, but Johnny agreed."

"He agreed? To let you walk away?" She bit her lip. "He's just as stupid as you. Must run in the family."

"Not exactly," I began. "I said I was thinking about leaving, and after I talked to him and gave the ultimatum, he saw my view."

"What?" she exclaimed. "What does that mean?"

"It means he knows I've had a few offers from other gyms, and a manager approached me as we were talking," I laughed.

"Oh, my freaking God! That's amazing!"

"Anyway, Johnny saw what was happening, especially after I told him the King's Alliance owner had already talked to me."

King's Alliance was the Rogue Warriors most known rival locally, and Johnny growled when I'd told him about the offer. I challenged him, and now he had to either let me go, or let Rachel back in.

"Oh, man!" She clapped her hands. "So, now what?"

"You're back in," I smiled.

"But I didn't earn it," she grimaced.

"Talk to Johnny." I pulled her into my arms and began kissing her neck. "You're back in the gym if you want it, and now, I want you to let me back in... to you, because I need it."

***

Six months later

Midway through the sparring match, I held up my hands. "Give me a minute."

"Can't take it, can you?" Rachel laughed.

"Shut the fuck up," I growled, taking my mouthpiece out of my mouth. I grabbed my water bottle and guzzled it.

"A few fight wins under his Featherweight belt, and he's letting a girl beat him," she chuckled.

"Got to hell," I quipped.

"Then come on!" She yelled. "Give it to me!"

"Oh, you know I will later," I joked.

Rachel rolled her eyes. "All talk and no action."

"Bitch!"

"Asshole!"

"What do ya say? We just get married! We act like we are already!"

"What? Are you freaking serious?" She dropped her hands, and I attacked.

I had her on the mat before she could say another word. I landed on top of her and stared into her eyes. "Marry me."

"Hell no," she shoved me off her, and stood. "That's the stupidest proposal anyone's ever done in the history of proposals!"

"Never claimed to be a fricking romantic," I stood.

"Ain't that the truth," she shook her head. "You're pathetic."

"Been called worse," I snorted.

"How about this?" she lowered her hands and sauntered closer. "We both win our next fights, and I'll marry you."

"Really?"

She nodded.

"You're on! Let's do this!"

9 781956 376197